NEW YORK M

This is a work of fiction. Names, characters, places and incidents are the products of the author's imagination. Any resemblance to actual events, locations, organisations or people, living or dead, is purely coincidental.

Copyright © 2024 by Stephen Aryan

All rights reserved. No part of this publication may be reproduced, circulated, stored in a retrieval system, or transmitted, in any form or by any means, without the prior permission in writing of the author. It may not be used to train AI under any circumstances.

STEPHEN ARYAN

For Scott

NEW YORK MINUTE

BY STEPHEN ARYAN

STEPHEN ARYAN

Other Books by Stephen Aryan

Age of Darkness
Battlemage
Bloodmage
Chaosmage

Age of Dread
Mageborn
Magefall
Magebane

Quest for Heroes
The Coward
The Warrior

The Nightingale and the Falcon
The Judas Blossom
The Blood Dimmed Tide

NEW YORK MINUTE

CHAPTER 1

I'd barely been awake five minutes when someone started pounding on the front door. Someone with a heavy, impatient hand. Glancing at my watch, I realised that it was a little after seven in the morning.

"Just a second."

I pulled on some pants, picked up a dagger, and shuffled into the main room. I could see the shadow of someone walking back and forth past the window. With the blade hidden, I cracked open the door and peered out.

Sunlight stabbed my eyes, gold and white spots danced, and when they'd faded, I saw the face of my early morning caller.

"Do you know what time it is?" I asked, staring at the big bald bastard lurking outside. He had a face that looked as if it had regular appointments with a shovel. Nose splashed flat, piggy eyes hidden beneath a forehead shelf, thick lantern jaw decorated with orange fuzz suggesting Irish blood. He was also ripped with muscle, probably from steroids. It looked as if he'd been badly put together from spare parts, like Frankenstein's monster. He was definitely hired muscle. The pressing question was, whose?

He shrugged, uncaring about the hour. "Are you Cole Blackstone?"

"Yeah."

"Boss wants to see you about a job. Said it's urgent."

"Who's your boss?"

"Dolman."

Fuck.

That's a name everyone in New York knows. Karl Dolman is a ruthless son of a bitch who is probably responsible for most of the drugs floating around the city. His businesses cover the usual — smuggling, gambling, prostitution — but drugs are where he excels.

About ten years back, Dolman hired a bunch of clever chemists who cooked up all kinds of new and weird concoctions from the local flora and fauna. Eventually they found something that was highly addictive, hallucinogenic, but with a low mortality rate. They called it Sky. Apart from a small chance of death, Sky leaves addicts with a glowing high which made it the new must-have drug for the trendies and those with money. A short time later, it was available from every street corner, bar, night club and dark alley. Soon Dolman had so much money he was able to build an empire.

His competition has been trying to crack the recipe for years, and the police are desperate to get Sky off the streets, but no one's made much progress.

Dolman and his gang, the Dragons, are known for being bloodthirsty. Axes are their weapon of choice, and they seem to enjoy chopping off people's hands and feet. Anyone caught stealing, or trying to encroach on Dolman's territory, loses a hand or foot. A living, shambling reminder is a better deterrent than a dead body which is soon forgotten.

Being a private investigator is a tough job at the best of times. It's made worse in a city as big as New York, with so many people and their problems. Normally I'm a bit choosier about my clients but, on this occasion, I knew I couldn't refuse. If Dolman knew my name and where I lived, then he already had too much information about me. A polite 'no thanks' could cost me a hand. A 'fuck you' could get me killed.

"Can I have a minute to get dressed?" I asked, tucking the knife into the back of my pants.

NEW YORK MINUTE

The big man thought about it. It took him a while. "Yeah. I guess so."

"Wanna come in?"

He considered it, working it through the thing that passed for a brain in his cavernous skull. "All right."

"You got a name?"

"Everyone has a name."

I took a deep breath, counted to five in my head, and tried again. "What's your name?"

"Caleb."

"Great. Take a seat, Caleb," I said gesturing at the couch before throwing open the curtains.

These days, I make a modest living, but my house is still nice. The benefits of a decent pension and a pay-off from the police a few years back. Most of the people who live this far south in the Brooklyn suburbs are young, or fairly well-to-do families with kids. I'm one of the few exceptions, but we get along just fine, as long as the kids don't leave their toys lying around where I'll trip over them.

The buildings are two or three storeys high, moulded from gel-plac, a durable grey substance like organic concrete. These days, no one has any idea how to make more of it, so we've stuck to bricks and wood. The buildings on my street are one family per floor, which is spacious and better than some in the inner city. A few choose to live in tiny cubicles they call micro-homes, and pay extortionate prices for the privilege of being inner-city dwellers. I'd rather live out here where it's green and quiet, even if it borders on the Wild.

I'm also lucky. There was a fire on the top floor of my building a few years ago, which destroyed it. The city authorities ripped out the second storey as well, so I have this place all to myself. So far, they haven't rebuilt the upper floors. It could still happen one day and shit all over my good fortune, but hopefully not.

Leaving chatty Caleb on the couch, I gestured at the bookshelves in case he wanted to do something while I went into the bathroom. Despite a decent night's sleep, the bags under my eyes were still there, purple slashes across my face. Maybe it's my age, because these days they seem to be permanent. Grey eyes that used to be bright blue. Olive skin from descendants who hailed from somewhere around the Mediterranean. A touch of grey in the stubble on my chin glares at me. The wound, from a knife years ago, healed. You'd have to look to find the scar, but the hair around it has never been right. It's a constant reminder that I trusted the wrong person at the wrong time. It's not a mistake that I'll repeat.

After splashing water on my face and running more through my hair, affectionately called salt and pepper by some, I run a bar of soap over my skin and rinse off. Black pants, a grey cotton shirt, and worn but comfortable leather boots used to walking long distances. Over the top goes my fur-lined jacket to keep out the chill, and then my belt.

As I entered the living room and picked up my Colt short sword, Caleb's eyes widened. One of his hands moved towards the custom-made hatchet on his belt.

"It's just a precaution. You know what the inner city is like."

He mulled it over and eventually sat back.

"Ready to go," I said.

According to my watch it was barely eight in the morning as we stepped outside. Despite the neighbourhood, I securely locked the front door and pocketed the key. If someone was determined, they could pick it, but I don't have much that's worth stealing. Some clothes and a few books, but there's no money or valuables in the house.

Glancing overhead there was still a touch of black and purple around the edges of the morning sky. The egg-heads would know the reason why it's like that. Trapped gas in the atmosphere or something. The two grey moons, Artemis and

NEW YORK MINUTE

Apollo, were still visible, one smooth and flat like a glass marble, the other fat and lumpy.

Far above, I saw a shimmer and then it was gone. A dying star. A comet. Who knows. I don't have the time or patience for stargazing. It's not going to change what's happening down here on the streets.

Caleb and I headed down tree-lined streets and I saw him glancing at the compacted earth. In the inner city, across all of Manhattan, Brooklyn, the Bronx, and part of Queens, the roads are paved with stone. There's no Staten Island here. That's the Old Country.

Everything old is new again, or at least, the parts of history we can stomach. The rest, our ancestors tried to leave behind, and good riddance. They made a mess of the Old Country. That's one of the reasons we're here in this new place, trying to do things right this time.

The city authorities keep talking about extending the paving this far, but they haven't got around to it. They have plenty of other things to focus on and they don't have the time or money, which is fine with me. I like the rustic country feeling, even though we're still within city limits. Ride an hour south, into the Wild, where it's really overgrown, and it couldn't be more different from the inner city. New York has streets and back alleys, where nothing grows and we've pushed wildlife to the fringes. People come first. Out there, it's a jungle. Nature rules and we're just squatting in her backyard.

It's funny. I came into the world in a hospital in Manhattan, not far from what we call Hell's Kitchen, but somewhere in my family's history, there's a bit of the countryside in my blood. I'm someone who likes trees over pavement. Yeah, I never saw it coming either.

In my youth, I was a city-rat, down to the marrow. The back alleys and side streets of New York were my playground. Glittering roads full of broken glass bottles. Paint-daubed corners where dealers took care of business. Stinking alleyways full of rotting food and vermin the size of cats. There were a hundred dangers all around, but they were familiar, and all of it was mine, and I wasn't scared.

The whole place was so deeply ingrained in me that I knew I'd never want to leave the inner city. A few decades later that turned out not to be true. Now, the quiet suits me over the noise of downtown. Funny thing is, I can't stomach the smell anymore. Out here in the suburbs, it's a different city. A different world.

When we got to the main road we headed north and the foot traffic started to pick up. Folk on carts laden with goods passed us at a steady clip heading into the city. The top of my head was almost on par with the stomach of their grey-green horses, and I'm not a short man by any measure.

It's this place, this new world. After a while, the horses were born big and their skin was kind of green, but for the most part, they're meek and gentle. It's only occasionally there's a wild one that's a throwback to something primal, like the beasts rumoured to exist in the heart of the Wild. The throwbacks can't be tamed, and they're quickly carted off before they maul someone.

The city authorities say such horses are put to death, or turned into glue, but I wonder. You could say it's part of my natural distrust of authority, or that I'm being paranoid, but what if I'm right and they're experimenting on them?

There's a lot that goes on that people don't know about. Most of the time, they don't want to know.

A short walk brought us to the nearest trolley stop heading into Manhattan. There was already a line of people waiting and, member of the Dragons or not, Caleb had to join me at the back of the queue. That early, they're inner-city workers happy to make the long commute. I noticed there was a mix of labourers for the mills, bartenders for the clubs, a couple of smiths, and a few well-to-do shopkeepers and engineers, their noses buried in technical books.

A few were wearing hats, but Caleb and I were the only ones with weapons in plain sight. Our blades received a couple of glances, but nothing more. I bet they all had a dagger or two somewhere stashed on their person. If they didn't then they were more stupid than they looked. The law does its best, but it can't be everywhere at once. These days, they only tend to solve crimes after the fact. Preventing them is too difficult and too dangerous. Besides, there are too many people and not enough police officers.

When the trolley arrived, pulled by four of the biggest horses I've ever seen, there was plenty of space for us to find a pair of seats. It would fill up the closer we got to the city centre, but that was all right. It would take almost an hour before we reached the end of the line, and that would give me time for a snooze. Urgent meeting with Dolman or not, I dozed off in no time.

A bump in the road woke me, and at first, I was disorientated. Caleb was still there beside me, silent and unblinking as he stared out the window. Coming into view on our left, surging along, blue and bright in the morning sun, was the Hudson. Beyond that are the fields. Seemingly endless fields of grain, vegetables, and meadows, where cattle are watched over by shepherds armed with crossbows. People work hard to raise livestock and thieves are never arrested. They tend to turn up dead, hung on crosses in the middle of fields like scarecrows. These days, there isn't a lot of cattle rustling.

There's also the risk of graumkins trying to steal a lamb or two. They're the local birds of prey that are about the size of vultures. Ugly things with black and white spots and vicious beaks curved for tearing meat. Nailing the corpse of one to a fencepost sends a clear message and, until it rots, the others tend to stay away. I spoke to a farmer once. He said it had something to with the smell, but I'm not sure. Graumkins are eerily smart.

This close to the city, there aren't many mountain lions, but occasionally one of them wanders out of the Wild. We've done our best to keep the worst at bay, but every now and then, we're reminded that Mother Nature is merciless and she only favours the strong.

Up ahead, I could already see the Sky Towers standing tall above the rest of the city. Eleven glass and metal needles scraping at the sky. Edifices to the Old Country and the old way of life. The promise of a future that no one really wanted. Everything else in the city is smaller, tidier, and less wasteful. The tallest building put up since the towers is six storeys high. More than that is just a lot of stairs and sore legs.

The first settlers saw this place as a second chance for humanity. An opportunity to do it right this time, but soon enough, they fell into familiar patterns, creating everything the same as it had been before. Technology. Buildings with thirty or forty floors. Instant communication. Factories and mass production. Trains, and even air travel.

The Architects, the original city authorities put in charge of New York, tried to go ahead with their plans. No one asked the people what they wanted. Unions were formed and the workers went on strike. It was at that point the Architects came to the shocking discovery. They couldn't do it all by themselves. Talks were held and, in the end, the technological dream of the Architects died. The people wanted a simpler life. The Architects wanted one more in keeping with the Old Country. The union had thousands. The Architects had fifty, so they lost and the people won.

The giant machines ground to a halt and the Archive, the well of all knowledge and the seed bank from the Old Country, was shut down. And we entered a new, golden age. Well, that's what we're taught at school. Some regard this as a new dark age, but fuck them.

There are rumours and conspiracy theories about where the Architects and their Archive went, but no one really knows. Some say they travelled to another continent and started over. Some say they all died out. Most of the stories sound like bullshit but, every now and then, one of them feels like it has a kernel of truth.

So, the Architects disappeared. A board of governors was elected and they became the new authority in the city. Despite the changes, some folk decided to leave New York. They walked off into the Wild and set up their own communities. Some thrived and eventually became cities with familiar names: London, Boston, Delhi, Canberra. Others didn't last for more than a generation or two before everyone died. Sometimes it was a new disease that we couldn't cure. Sometimes it was fighting with their neighbours. Sometimes they just disappeared. It's what happened to Sydney. One week a merchant found a thriving community, and the next, a ghost town with food on the table and hungry pigs in the yard.

Many of the people in those communities just wanted to live in peace, away from the noise of New York. Away from any kind of bureaucracy. These days, I can sympathise.

Sometimes rules are comforting. Other times, they're like a rope, choking the good out of you. Forcing you towards a path that feels wrong, deep in your gut.

There are more settlements out there in the Wild than people realise. Not that many in the city look past the ends of their noses. Good or bad, people tend to stick with what they know, even when there are other places to live. Not that I'm one to talk. I've never travelled further out than where I live in the suburbs. Maybe one day I'll take a trip into the Wild and see what's out there.

Yeah, right.

So here we are. New York city. A place like no other:

striving to be good, drowning in its own filth, going sour under the weight of so many bodies. There's my optimism again.

In need of distraction I turned to the big man.

"Do you know what all this is about?" I said.

At first, Caleb said nothing. When he eventually spoke, his tone was sombre. "The boss didn't say, but I can tell he's worried," said Caleb, which made me raise an eyebrow.

Maybe my first impression of chatty Caleb had been a little harsh. I couldn't see a man like Dolman talking about his feelings, let alone with the hired muscle. Either whatever was on Dolman's mind was so bad that he'd been throwing furniture in a tantrum, or the big man had known his boss long enough to recognise when something was wrong.

"Are you from the Kitchen?" I asked.

"Born and raised."

"I figured."

He was quiet for a time. Before, I would have said that Caleb was counting the freckles on his arms, but now I wondered if he was mulling things over. Maybe it just took him a bit longer than most people. He stared at the glass towers in the distance.

"Will you help him?" he asked.

I could have pointed out that I didn't really have a choice. That he'd roused me from my bed and that I was smart enough to be terrified of his bastard of a boss. That Dolman would have no regrets about ordering my death if I refused to help, or that Caleb would probably be the one to kill me.

I could have said all of that and more, but I didn't. Caleb knew who his boss was and his capabilities.

Instead, I swallowed the bitterness and bile, forced a smile and said, "Maybe."

NEW YORK MINUTE

CHAPTER 2

When the trolley reaches the edge of Brooklyn, it's the end of the line. Everyone got off and we started walking. We could have called for a cab but, after sitting around for so long, both of us needed to stretch our legs.

It was just after nine in the morning, businesses were setting up and the daytime smells of the city were beginning to rise. Coffee, freshly baked bread, bacon and eggs. I think we've been eating and drinking the same stuff for centuries at this point, in the Old Country and the new.

At night it smelled of alcohol, stale piss, frying meat, tobacco, blood and disappointment. New York was also a lot more dangerous in the dark. There weren't exactly no-go areas, but those with any common sense stayed away from certain neighbourhoods. There were also places where people could go to gamble, score drugs, and find company for an hour or more, if they were feeling energetic.

The police did their best to keep the peace, but they can't be everywhere. They don't have the bodies and they have to prioritise solving certain crimes. Murders are always ahead of theft and other small-time offences. That's why most people carry steel to discourage others from trying to take advantage. It isn't the Wild West of old, not by a long shot, but something needs to change or New York will become truly lawless, ruled by fear and brute force. Most of the time, it feels like the police are just another gang.

In the day, the city looked cleaner, more wholesome. It's as if the sunlight can undo mistakes and wash away the blood. I smelled fresh bread, hot metal, roasted coffee and the clean burn of citrus fruit. The repetitive strike of a hammer came from a smithy on my left. The heart of the forge glowed bright orange, like an infernal eye.

Even this far into the city, the streets were already filled with people in a rush. People late for work, mostly. Shopkeepers stood in doorways, calling out to those passing by. A few beckoned me towards their premises and I was tempted, but Caleb's expression soon put them off. I was already hungry and a little thirsty. The thought of a fresh cup of coffee and maybe a pastry was appealing, but Caleb wouldn't stop.

Urgent business called and he didn't want to be late. Refused to be. Blame, or perhaps guilt about whatever had happened, hung over him like a funeral shroud. His strides lengthened the closer we came to our destination, the heart of Manhattan.

Unlike the Old Country, there isn't a big park at the centre of New York. Why bother when the Wild beyond the city limits is one huge, savage garden? Instead, at the centre of Manhattan, is where it all began. The first buildings were built here, made in the old way with machinery and cranes, with guidance from the Architects. Once, the towers had housed the city's authorities, but they moved out a long time ago, or maybe they were forced out. I forget. I'm a bit shaky on early New York history.

These days, the posers and the rich are the only ones who can afford the extortionate rent. You can't own one of the towers. Not even Dolman. One day he'll be gone and the towers will still be here, making the horizon look untidy, scratching at the sky.

As we got closer to what many called the Squat Tower, a mere fourteen storeys high, I craned my neck but the top was out of sight. Some of the other towers are taller, but no one lives above the tenth or twelfth floor on any of them. It wasn't worth the hassle and no amount of money would persuade people to carry furniture up that many stairs. A couple of them had installed dumbwaiters to haul up small goods, but even that was an expensive luxury.

About a hundred years back, a plaintiff tried to sell the authorities on the idea of electricity. The problem was that it required an awful lot of tearing things up, planting thousands of wooden posts and making miles of conductive wire. Then you needed a huge power plant that had to constantly be fed with something to burn. To most folks, it seemed like an awful lot of work, never mind the destruction. Everyone had been managing just fine with oil lamps, wood and candles up to that point. So the plaintiff was told to go away and find something better to do with his time. And ever since then, we've been doing it our own way, with oil and wood.

The paved streets felt wrong under my boots. The dull echo of my heels made me feel disconnected from the earth. It's like a hard scab had been laid over the world, trying to keep out what's real. Through a crack in the stone, I spotted a tiny green weed with purple flowers that had pushed its way up. It made me smile and Caleb caught me staring, apparently at nothing. Turnaround is fair. He probably thought I was simple-minded.

"What floor?" I asked, hoping it wasn't too far up. I've never liked heights.

"Fourteenth," he said. Of course. It had to be the top floor. A man like Dolman would want the penthouse.

"Lead on," I said, trying not to sigh about the climb.

The ground floor lobby was dirty, scoured by the wind, stripped to the bones, making the building feel seedy and disreputable. It's a far cry from its heyday as the central hub of power in the city, where those in charge made decisions that would affect the rest of us for generations to come. If they were still alive today, I wonder what they'd make of the city and its people. Would they be angry at us for squatting in the ruins and never fulfilling their dream of a sparkling metropolis? Or would they be proud of all that we've accomplished and applaud our ingenuity and ability to say no? My gut tells me the former. I've never met a man or woman in charge who wasn't some kind of bastard.

As we crawled up the stained and pitted concrete stairs it began to feel like we were ants trekking through the gullet of some enormous beast. Recessed lights in the walls drove back the gloom enough to stop me tripping over my feet, but the shadows were still thick in the corners. The technology, something to do with the sun tiles on the roof, was starting to break down. Soon they'll be back to candles and lanterns like the rest of us.

Locked inside the building, the pleasant morning smells of the city started to fade. Instead, there was a host of other smells that had soaked into the floor and walls over the years. Abrasive, painful smells that scratched the back of my throat. A tangled mess of things I didn't want to imagine.

How vicious does a crime have to be for it to imprint a smell on concrete?

Finally, we reached the fourteenth floor, and by then my legs were aching. Four heavily armed guards were waiting beside a thick set of double doors at the far end of the corridor. All the other doors on the fourteenth had been sealed off, so that there was only one way to enter Dolman's home. Each of the four thugs was wearing padded armour and had a scutum, a waist-high Roman-style shield, sat on the floor in front of them. Four spears leaned against the wall, and each guard had a crossbow held loosely at their waist. They pointed their bows at me as we reached the landing. Even the sight of Caleb didn't make them relax.

"Stay here," said Caleb, and I was more than happy to oblige. If one of the guards had an itchy trigger finger, I could end up skewered to the wall by accident.

NEW YORK MINUTE

Caleb casually walked towards them, seemingly without a care in the world. After a short but heated conversation, the guards relaxed and he waved me forward. The four guards eyed me with suspicion so I offered my sword even before they asked for it. One of the guards patted me down and found my retirement present, a punching dagger, tucked into the back of my belt. I'd forgotten it was there. He ground his teeth and I shrugged, waiting to see what would happen next. I was at their mercy, so whatever was going to happen would happen. There wasn't a lot I could do about it, fourteen floors up and without a pair of wings.

A second guard, another man, did another thorough search that made me feel like he should have bought me a drink first. He didn't smile, but I think he enjoyed it too much. Confident that I wasn't holding anything else, they let me pass and I followed Caleb through the ridiculously thick wooden doors. On the rear of the door, I noticed metal hooks and a huge crossbar. If Dolman wanted, he could make this place into an impenetrable fortress.

Inside, the bare walls had been covered with wooden panelling which someone had painted a disturbing shade of red. It did nothing to dispel my notion that we were traversing the interior of some huge beast. Thankfully there was plenty to distract me from that line of thought. Thick, warm curtains, trimmed with gold thread, covered the large windows making it feel quite homely. Rather plain, but probably very expensive, watercolour paintings hung on the walls at regular intervals. Spaced out between them were artefacts on marble pedestals. Peculiar lumps of metal bent into shapes I found baffling and their purpose unknowable. In one glass case sat what looked like a mechanical heart, a fist-sized lump of blue-green steel sprouting wires like veins and arteries. Maybe the stories of artificial steel men in the Old Country were true after all.

The only way to know what any of it is for would be to

access the Archive, and those in charge of it aren't about to share. It's the most highly guarded secret in New York because no one knows where it went once the Architects moved out of the towers. There are hundreds of theories, but no one has ever come close to discovering its location.

Caleb had seen Dolman's artefacts many times and wasn't distracted. From the end of the corridor, he gestured for me to follow him into the next room. As soon as I walked in, everyone's eyes widened with surprise. Clearly I wasn't expected, not by Dolman nor his children, who were just sitting down to breakfast.

The room was comfortable, welcoming, and it felt regularly used by the family. The large dining table was marked with rings and scratches. The wooden floor scuffed from chairs and feet. The leather on the green chairs before the fireplace was so old it'd begun to crack. Most impressive were the bookshelves jammed with leather-bound tomes, another display of Dolman's significant wealth.

One wall was almost completely taken up with huge glass windows that looked out at the city. It had been a long time since I'd seen it from this height, sprawled in all directions with its neat rows of houses and shops. I could see how it easy it would be for someone to get used to this view and the inherent dangers that came with it. Feeling superior, viewing everyone else as nothing more than ants to be squashed.

Dolman was a man somewhere in his fifties, grey around the temples, squat and broad with arms hairy enough to impress a bear. I didn't want to imagine what his back and chest looked like. His untidy moustache, tousled hair and silk robe suggested he'd not been awake for long. At first glance, he resembled a hundred other men I'd seen. Men who'd become fathers later in life, who then spent an inordinate amount of time running after small children. But there was a lot more to Dolman than what was on the surface. He was a monster. Probably the worst the city had ever seen. A vicious man with unparalleled ambition and the intelligence to turn it into a reality.

Two children at the table, a cute blonde girl of about five with pigtails and a button nose, and a dark-haired brooding boy of maybe seven. The lad resembled his father, right down to the emerald green eyes, and the girl presumably favoured the mother, some young blonde beauty. As if my thoughts had summoned her, a willowy woman, at least twenty years Dolman's junior, came into the breakfast room dressed in a pink robe and slippers.

"Who is that and why is he at the breakfast table?" she asked, pointing one manicured finger at me.

Dolman looked at his wife and they both turned towards Caleb who had been lurking beside his boss.

"You said it was urgent," said the big man, by way of apology.

Dolman blinked a few times and then scrunched up his eyes. I imagined he was counting to five in his head. It seemed like a regular thing with Caleb. "That was late last night. I said we'd deal with it today."

Caleb shrugged. "I set off straight away."

"Did he get you out of bed?" asked Dolman, turning towards me.

"Yeah, he did."

"My apologies," said Dolman, gesturing at the empty chair on his left. His wife sat on his right, beside the angelic little girl. "Caleb is very literal."

"I've noticed," I said, sitting next to the boy, who continued to glare at me, fork raised halfway towards his mouth.

"We can talk after breakfast," said Dolman, gesturing at the spread on the table. There were pancakes, fried eggs, bacon, sausages, a pot of coffee and plenty of toast and butter. It was better than I was used to and too good to refuse. My rumbling stomach was in agreement and made itself known to everyone in the room.

I helped myself to a big plate and happily ignored everyone as I shovelled food into my mouth, trying not to make too many orgasmic sounds. The family made idle chit-chat and thankfully no one tried to involve me in their conversations. This was a clear violation of Dolman's family time, so we all pretended I wasn't there.

Once I'd eaten my fill and drank two mugs of coffee, I felt better and more alert. If nothing else, at least I'd had a delicious last meal. Hopefully it wouldn't come to that, but it was always good to be prepared for the worst.

The family finished eating and the wife, who no one had introduced, left the room with the little ones in tow. What remained on the plates was taken away by a sheepish Caleb, leaving me alone with the boss. We sat together in silence and I felt him studying me. If I were twenty years younger, or more insecure, I might have fidgeted. But this wasn't the first time I'd been in danger or been alone in a room with a scary man.

My earlier assessment of Dolman as a caring family man wasn't inaccurate, but without them in the room, it was easier to see the other side of him. It was as if all the love and kindness he'd displayed earlier was sinking beneath his skin, like sediment to the bottom of a glass of beer. It didn't take too long to see the ruthless, notorious leader of a business empire built on blood and misery.

"My first wife gave me two children when we were young," he said, out of nowhere. "A boy and a girl. Tony is my heir, my pride and joy. What's that old saying? A chip off the old block."

So that meant a murdering maniac and possible psychopath, just like dear old dad. Tony sounded like someone I didn't want to meet in a dark alley. I wondered if he was telling me this to generate sympathy for his predicament. If so, it wasn't working.

"My daughter, Selina, is different. Always wanted to do things her own way. At first, it terrified me. She was always causing problems, getting into trouble, but then I realised that she was an entrepreneur. Tony is a good boy, there's no doubt. Smart, up to a point. One day, he'll take over and the business will do just fine. Selina…"

For a moment I thought Dolman was going to cry. Instead his hands curled into fists, and I immediately leaned back from the churning river of rage behind his eyes.

There he was.

The butcher and architect of at least two gang massacres. There was more blood on his hands than any veteran butcher who spent their days up to the elbows in animal carcases.

"Someone has taken my Selina, and you are going to find out who." It was a statement. We both knew that I had to take the job or learn how to fly.

I let his words sit for a while, giving him time to cool off. Slowly, his hands uncurled and he ran one through his hair in a vague attempt to flatten the unruly tangle.

"When was she taken?"

"Two days ago. She has her own place on the third floor, but I still see her every day. Even if it's just for a few minutes. She's got her own businesses, investments to check on, but we always talk. When she didn't show up yesterday I wasn't too worried. Last night I was concerned, so I sent Booker down to check up on her. The lock hadn't been tampered with, but inside was a mess. Dents in the walls, broken glass, pieces of furniture. There was some blood, but not much, so they wanted her alive."

So she'd opened the door to a familiar face and something had gone terribly wrong. Either she'd been betrayed by one of her friends or they'd turned on her, probably for a fat wad of cash. Either way it didn't look good for Selina.

"What else can you tell me about her? Even the small stuff could be helpful." I didn't want to pry, as I'd already stepped into his personal space, but the more he could tell me, the better.

"Booker will give you a picture," he said, waving a hand to dismiss me.

"Where does she normally go day to day? Does she have a boyfriend? Girlfriend? What about her friends?"

Dolman stared at me and I had the distinct feeling he was thinking about throwing me out the window. It would be an interesting way to go, and one I'd not spent much time considering. Despite the view, it wasn't one that I fancied trying.

He didn't need me to remind him that I was here at his behest. In situations like this, I've found silence to be my best weapon, that and trying not to look threatening.

"She likes food. That's why she put some of her money into restaurants. Most evenings she goes to some clubs to relax, Booker can tell you which ones. I don't know about her friends or anyone in her life." I could hear the regret in his voice and I looked away, in case I started to feel sympathy for him. Despite the silk robe, comfy chairs and sweet little kids, he was still a murdering bastard.

For all of his self-delusion, Dolman was beginning to realise he didn't know his eldest daughter all that well. Perhaps it was because he'd been spending more time with his new wife and second brood.

Dolman began to fidget and I knew my time was almost up. "Final question. Why me? Why not send one of your own people?"

"I have rivals out there. Gangs that are trying to slice off a piece of my business. They have eyes and ears everywhere. They know my people and if some of them start asking questions, it could be seen as weakness. I can't take the risk."

"What if one of them is responsible for taking her?"

"You just need to find out who. Leave the rest to me."

I had no doubt what would happen after that. A lot of

blood. Corpses washing up in the river for days. Stinking, fly-ridden piles of body parts littering the streets.

Dolman stood, signalling that our meeting was over, and I stepped away from the table, wiping my mouth with a napkin.

"Find my girl. You'll be handsomely rewarded."

Of that, I had no doubt, as long as I was successful. I wondered what would happen if I found her and she was already dead. There was an old saying about not killing the messenger, but I couldn't see Dolman playing nice for the sake of tradition.

Now, it was a matter of life or death.

CHAPTER 3

I found Caleb waiting outside the dining room in the corridor. He was leaning against the wall with his head tipped back and eyes closed. At first I thought he was asleep, or dead, until he heard my footsteps. Caleb came back to life, watching me with slow-blinking eyes. I think he had been up all night.

"You need to get some sleep and I need to talk to someone called Booker before I go."

Caleb mulled it over and then waved one meaty hand for me to follow him. We went down a couple of flights of stairs and then along a warren of corridors to a tidy office. I expected Booker to be an accountant of some kind, but he turned out to be another muscled-up beefcake. Where Caleb was in the prime of life, Booker was a man well past his middle years. He was short and broad with arms as thick as my legs, but some of his bulk was turning to fat. The wrinkles on his bald head were more prominent because of his lack of hair, and the small, round spectacles perched on the end of his nose were comical. I would have laughed if not for the whole situation. Instead, I bit the inside of my mouth and waited to be introduced.

"Ah, Blackstone," he said, before Caleb had a chance to find the words. "Take a seat."

The office was small, and from Booker's smart trousers, freshly pressed shirt and immaculate nails, I could tell he was a neat freak. Caleb closed the door behind him and sloped off, probably to get some sleep. I felt Booker studying me as I glanced around the room. A desk, two chairs, bookcases full of files and a couple of lanterns for working late at night. The stubs of several brightly coloured candles sat on top of one bookshelf. It explained why the room smelled of lemon and a hint of lavender, instead of mouldy paper and old farts. On the back of the door was a small painting of a teenage girl with dark hair. She was probably a relative. It was faded and worn around the edges, suggesting it had been hanging there for some time. It wasn't much, but Booker had made the office his own.

"Dolman said you could tell me something about Selina. Where does she go? Who are her friends? That kind of thing."

"Can I ask you something first?" said Booker. I noticed there was a slight drawl to his words, as if he'd only recently learned how to talk. Although there weren't any visible signs on his face, I guessed something had popped in his head a while back causing a minor stroke. Maybe that was why someone of his considerable bulk was working behind a desk for Dolman.

"Seems fair," I said, having a good idea about what was coming.

"Didn't you use to be a cop?"

"That was a long time ago."

It wasn't something I liked to talk about. The circumstances surrounding my early retirement were not well-known, and I wasn't keen on dredging up the past. There's an old saying about time healing all wounds but I think that's crap. We just get used to carrying around a certain amount of pain.

In my opinion, the best thing you can do is get busy living so you don't have time to waste thinking about what could have been. That way leads to madness, regret, and a lot of drinking.

"These days I'm a freelance PI. I've been my own boss for a few years."

Booker grunted. "We all do crazy shit when we're young."

"That's true."

"Selina has a lot of secrets. Most she doesn't share, but there are a couple of big ones that nearly everyone knows," said

Booker, pointing at the ceiling and daddy dearest a couple of floors up. "The kind of thing he'd frown on."

"Like what?"

"She frequents clubs that only cater to women."

I wasn't surprised that Dolman was against that sort of thing. He struck me as an old-fashioned guy who favoured traditional family values. He'd already spoken about his son, Tony, being his pride and joy. It was a good thing for Dolman that his heir liked women instead of men.

"Is that a problem for you?" asked Booker.

I shrugged. "Doesn't bother me."

"Whatever makes her happy, I say. You got kids?"

"No. Anything else you can tell me about her?" I said, steering Booker back on track.

I was starting to get the feeling Booker was lonely from working by himself all day, but I wasn't there to be his new best friend. From the fading scars on his hands and face, I knew he'd hurt and probably killed people for Dolman. Booker was a middle-aged, overweight man, but despite his pleasant demeanour and open-minded attitude, I knew he was a killer. It was there, behind his eyes. He'd mentioned doing crazy things when he was young and I didn't want to know. As a rule I don't make friends with murderers.

Booker took the hint, sucked his teeth, which were remarkably intact, and jotted down an address. "Try this club. Someone there will know her, or if not, what other clubs to try."

"Do you have a picture?"

Booker fished out a small charcoal sketch of Selina from his desk drawer. She was a good-looking young woman, but there was something about her broody eyes that I didn't like. They reminded me too much of her father.

"What about friends? Does she have a girlfriend?" I asked.

"Not that I know of, but these days she doesn't come

around much to chat."

"Thanks for the info," I said, before Booker tried to tell me more about his sad little life.

I'd seen plenty of men and women like him and Dolman before. Caring, affectionate, and capable of love when it came to their own flesh and blood. They were the kind of people who would kiss their child in one room and then walk into the next and smash someone's head without missing a beat. I understood them, on occasion could even empathise with or admire them, but I never wanted to be their friend.

"I hope you find her," said Booker. He sounded genuine, but it was hard to tell.

Giving myself time for my thoughts to settle, I set a steady pace going back down the stairs. There was a lot going on, more than anyone realised. Dolman was in the dark about his daughter, and although Booker had a better idea of who she was, he'd said there was much she kept from him. Selina had grown up and gone her own way, and so far, no one had been able to name a single friend. It seemed as if she had a secret life. Something that was completely her own. A whole world that she kept separate from her father and everything that came with his name.

By time the time I made it down to the street, my legs were burning but I was intrigued about the case. We'd not talked terms, but I didn't think Dolman was going to skimp on my daily rate.

I didn't know this part of the city very well, but after only a short walk I found a quiet little coffee shop to mull things over. I took a table outside on the pavement, sipped my coffee, and watched the world go by.

If one of Dolman's rivals had grabbed his daughter, they might try to use her as a bargaining chip in their war. Get him to back off territory, agree to some kind of a deal, or they'd send her back to him in pieces. A guy like Dolman, he'd baulk at being manipulated, and wouldn't like the bruise to his pride. Maybe he'd change his mind after the first few fingers, maybe he wouldn't. Maybe he'd hold out long enough to leave her a cripple before finally agreeing to the terms. And maybe he'd just send all of his people out to kill and keep going until they found those responsible.

On the surface, a war between criminal gangs didn't sound like a bad thing. They had signed up for bloodshed and violence, and none of them were saints, except that it was never that clean cut. Innocent people always got hurt. They weren't the target but someone would end up in the wrong place at the wrong time.

The only thing I could do to try and avoid the bloodshed was find Selina, work out who was manipulating who and why. Hopefully there was enough wiggle room in there for me to escape with my skin intact. It wasn't much of a plan, but it was all I had.

As I was heading for the address Booker had given me, I heard someone approaching in a hurry. Glancing over my shoulder, I saw a young man running with a cosh raised above his head. Waiting until the last second, I jerked to one side and stuck out my foot. He tripped and went skidding down the street on his face.

Someone else came at me, a burly young woman with short red hair and freckles. I might have thought her cute if not for the baton in her hand and her vicious grin. She swung at my head and I backed up until I was against a wall with nowhere to go. She tried again and this time, I took the blow on my forearm which went numb. Before she had a chance to pull out of range, I jabbed her in the face and felt her nose break. Hooking one knee with my foot, I shoved and she fell, smacking the back of her head on the paved ground.

Two more people appeared, armed with wooden clubs. Someone was desperate to have a chat with me, otherwise they would have drawn a blade by now. As I was readying myself, I heard a tell-tale click coming from my left.

"That's enough," said a wheezy voice. An older man with badly pock-marked skin was pointing a crossbow at me. "Will you come quietly?"

The others were embarrassed, bleeding and angry at being given a beating by someone more than twice their age, but he was calm. Without being asked, I held out my sword and punching dagger. One of the younger thugs snatched them off me and did a thorough search.

"He's clean, Duke," said the young guy.

"Nice and easy, now," said Duke, jerking his head to the right. I knew the younger thugs wanted to hurt me, but they held back and followed his orders. I went as directed, taking narrow alleys and quiet streets while Duke followed at a distance. If I ran, he'd put a bolt between my shoulder blades.

Two of the youngsters roamed ahead, clearing the way of nosy pedestrians. A short time later, I was directed towards a warehouse. I noticed the lock on the door had been broken. Whoever wanted to speak with me was being cautious, which showed that they had some intelligence. But given how they had approached me, I didn't think it was an abundance of intelligence. There were nicer and quieter ways to arrange a private chat.

The warehouse was full of wooden crates stacked floor to ceiling. It smelled of rain and something earthy. There was an office at one end, and sat outside in a pool of his own blood, was a middle-aged man. I guessed he was the owner, or at least someone who had worked in the warehouse. I took a deep breath and moved on, knowing it was already too late for him.

Waiting for me inside the office, sitting behind the cheap wooden desk like a king on his throne, was a weasel-faced man with red hair and beady eyes. His nose was so long and bent it almost touched his top lip, and half of his left ear was missing.

It had been sliced off at some point, suggesting he'd been part of this life for some time.

"Who are you? Why were you visiting Dolman?" he asked without preamble.

Taking my time, I sat opposite, rearranged my coat and made myself comfortable. I tried to be the picture of someone at ease. "Who are you?" I asked in return.

I sensed someone moving behind me but weasel-face shook his head. No doubt one of the young bloods had been about to knock me out of my chair to teach me some manners. I'd seen it all before. That sort of bluster and intimidation didn't impress me. Not one fucking bit.

"I'm Felix, and this is my gang. We're the Warlords," he said, feigning a smile. "Your turn."

"I'm a PI. I'm doing a job for Dolman."

Felix twitched as I mentioned the big man's name. It was a small tell, but I knew despite his attempts to look nonchalant, Dolman made him nervous.

"What kind of job?"

"I can't tell you. It's a private matter. Maybe you should ask him."

"We could make you tell us," said Felix, and I felt a couple of people looming over me from behind.

"Boy, let me make something abundantly clear, since it seems to have escaped your notice. I'm not scared of you or any of your piss-poor gang of inbred teenagers. If not for Duke, I would have taught the rest of your foot soldiers a lesson about respect."

I was poking him on purpose, playing tough to see which way he'd blow, hot or cold. Felix was the leader of this rag-tag group. So that meant he was there for a reason. Usually it came down to having something between his ears other than rage and a hard-on for violence. Those kinds of people tended to take a long time to get warmed up. Of course there was also the other kind of leader. The maniac who was so scary no one wanted to challenge them. The kind who'd kill their own mother if they thought she was disrespecting them. Thankfully my instincts were right. He fell into the first category.

Felix looked past me at someone in the back of the room and raised an eyebrow. "He's right," said Duke. "He was giving them all a good beating."

"We had him," said another, younger, voice. Duke guffawed and Felix stepped in before it escalated.

"Give us a minute," he said, dismissing everyone. "Duke, you stay."

The rest of the Warlords shuffled out. Duke closed the door and leaned against it, the crossbow held down at his side.

"I'm going to tell you about an interesting rumour I heard yesterday." Felix put his feet up on the desk and leaned back in his chair. I noticed blood on the soles of both shoes.

"Talk all you want. I'm not telling you why I was there."

"I think you were hired to find Dolman's daughter. I heard she's not been seen for days." Felix was grinning but I kept my expression neutral and maintained an air of boredom. "I've had my people watching the Squat Tower since, but there's been no sign of her. What do you think of that?"

"I think you need a new hobby. Maybe a girlfriend."

What I actually thought was far less kind. Felix and his Warlords were amateurs. So far, everything about how they operated told me they were wannabes trying to bite off a piece of someone else's territory. They were nothing more than hoodlums with aspirations, and the only ballast keeping them on course was Duke. He was old enough to know better, but I suspected he'd been turfed out of another gang and was trying to build something new. Felix was the pilot, steering the ship, but Duke was the Captain, navigating the water ahead and probably making all the plans in secret.

"I think Dolman is worried, so he hired you to find her,"

said Felix, getting into his stride. "He doesn't want to look weak in front of his enemies. If he can't protect his own daughter, what does that say about him?"

Felix was right about one thing: it didn't look good for Dolman.

"How much is your daily rate?" he asked, reaching into his pocket.

"Two hundred."

"And how long, on average, would a hypothetical missing person case take to solve?"

"About two weeks," I said with a shrug.

"All right," said Felix, counting out a stack of notes from a fat wad. "There's three grand. Two weeks and a little extra." As he pushed the money across the table I noticed the dried blood under his fingernails. "I'm paying you to not do your job. Take a couple of weeks off. Go to the pub, take a holiday, stay home and jerk off. Whatever. I don't care. Just stay away, for two weeks. That's a good deal, right?"

"I think so."

"Then we have an understanding?" said Felix, offering another smile.

"Sure," I said, forcing a smile. He offered his hand to make the deal and I shook it. It took a great deal of effort not to rip off his arm and beat him to death with it. I picked up the money and stuffed it in a pocket which made Felix grin.

"See, I told you, Duke," said Felix, smiling at his mentor. "You just have to treat people with a bit of respect and they'll come around."

Duke didn't say anything. I doubt I'd convinced him, but he stepped away from the door and let me leave the office. One of the young Warlords, the girl with the broken nose, handed back my weapons. She was biting her lower lip, desperate to say something cutting, but someone had told her to play nice. I almost commented about the busted nose improving her looks, but resisted the urge. They were young, angry and hungry for violence, with a thin line of authority holding them back. At some point, Duke's control over them would slip and I didn't want to be around to see what happened next.

When I was a few streets away from the warehouse I stopped to make sure I wasn't being followed, then took a long and winding route just to be safe.

Felix and his Warlords wanted Dolman to look weak. They were hoping that his family problems would keep him distracted long enough for them to carve out some territory for themselves. If that happened, it would make others doubt Dolman. They might begin to question his position at the top of the food chain, and that would lead to more gang violence.

The situation was escalating faster than I'd anticipated. I had the horrible feeling that no matter what I did, there would be blood on the streets. I needed help. Someone I could trust to watch my back, no matter the odds. I had a short list of friends to begin with and there was only one person I knew I could rely on: my oldest friend, Bracken Hart.

CHAPTER 4

If big green horses and the occasional kid going missing in the Wild were all that we had to worry about in the New Country, there wouldn't be much to complain about. But this place had a number of surprises that no one could have predicted. It wasn't as if the Archive could help either, because the problems were new, not old. One of them is the Slate.

I've known Bracken nearly all my life. We weren't close as kids, but by the time we turned ten, we were like brothers. To look at us, you wouldn't think it. His skin is kind of dusky and he has big blocky features, as if he has been carved from stone or old wood. Dark eyes, dark hair and a solid build with heavy shoulders. Bracken isn't the kind of person you want to meet in a bad mood.

His ancestors were tribespeople from the North American plains, with old-fashioned ideas and ancient rituals. Most of them in the New Country don't bother with the old ways. Bracken was made different. He was serious from a young age and so quiet, his parents thought he was short in the head. It turned out he didn't speak, not because he couldn't, but because he didn't have anything to say. Over the years, he's loosened up with me, but not much with others.

Unlike me, Bracken was only ever interested in one woman. He grew from a quiet teenager into a solid and reliable man, skilled with his hands, patient and caring. Margot was the love of his life, still is I guess, even though it's been five years since she died. It was nobody's fault. A sickness we can't cure took her. They were together for many years before and she blessed him with two girls. Marie and Gert. I've been an uncle to them since the moment they were born. I know you're not supposed to have favourites, but I'm not their blood, so I can pick mine without feeling too guilty.

Marie is too much like her dad, quiet and serious, especially since her mother died. Gert is something else. Wild and glorious and so funny, with a dark and slightly twisted sense of humour. I miss them desperately.

A month ago, Bracken had to suddenly leave his job. His boss of twenty-five years didn't understand. Bracken was due to take over and run the whole operation when the old girl retired, but that wasn't possible anymore. Not since he got the Slate.

It's incurable and fatal. Occasionally, it happens quick, but that's rare. If you let it run its course, the Slate will kill an adult in about two years. Most people never last that long. It's common for the afflicted to take their own life rather than suffer through the symptoms. The only good thing about the Slate is that's not communicable, but that doesn't stop people from ostracising those with it.

Old bad habits are new again.

If I believed in any of the stuff the preachers waffle on about, I'd ask what kind of a God—or Gods—would do something so cruel. Kill the girls' mother and then set it up so that they would lose their dad early as well. But I've never been a believer, and I know it's all a load of horse shit. Stories meant to keep people quiet and happy. Make them compliant and, even worse, not cause a fuss when things go wrong. It also gives them someone that can never take responsibility or make up for what they've done.

Putting Felix and his idiots to the back of my mind, I set off for Bracken's home in the far north of Manhattan. Washington Heights used to be nice, but these days it's become rundown. Once the area was chic and modern, but as those with money moved away to live closer to the centre, the houses were left to rot. Families moved in and did their best to stop them falling down, but often they didn't have the cash to turn it from shabby into structurally sound.

Bracken's home is cheap and big and the rent is low. As I walked down the street, passed peeling paint, rusted signs and dead plants on the doorsteps, it was easy to see which was Bracken's half of the street. All but a couple of the houses were clean, tidy, and well-maintained.

Bracken was perched on the roof of a wide terraced house like a grisly gargoyle, his feet dangling over the edge. Building homes had been his life's work before he left his job. Now he does whatever work he can to improve the neighbourhood, sometimes without pay. Most of his neighbours would rather hire him than some idiot who doesn't know what they're doing with a hammer and nails. Bracken is improving the street, one house at a time. A strong wind could come through and not one slate would fly off and every building would stay upright. Even without the girls, the street will be one hell of a legacy for him to leave behind.

Bracken looked up as I approached, a hammer in one hand, nails in the other. Without ropes or scaffolding, I'd be scared shitless to be up that high in case I slipped and fell, but it doesn't bother him. Not much does these days, and that's part of the problem.

"Social call?" he said, getting straight to the point. We didn't bother with banter and bullshit. We'd known each other far too long for that dance.

"I've got a job."

"Uh." Bracken always managed to put numerous emotions into few words. It sounded like he was wondering if the job paid well and if it was going to be dangerous. I only had a little blood on me from the Warlords, but he noticed that and the marks on my hands from throwing them around.

NEW YORK MINUTE

"How long?" he asked.

"A week. Maybe less. Come down and we'll talk. It pays well."

"I need a minute," he said, putting two more nails in the roof with smooth, practised strikes. "There's beer in the larder."

I walked up the street to his house, a terrace he'd split with an old neighbour. She couldn't handle the stairs and these days he didn't need much space. So he'd converted downstairs into an apartment for her, and he lived in the upper floor. I waved to Mrs Van der Berg and forced a smile, even though the old hag hated me for some reason. I'd never been anything but kind and polite to her and all I got in return was venom and biting comments.

The old biddy sneered at me and, for a second, I thought she was going to spit on my shoes. Instead, she turned back to her knitting. It was a brightly coloured scarf or jumper for one of her many fat, ugly grandchildren.

Upstairs in the stone-lined larder, I fished out a couple of bottles of beer. There isn't much to see in Bracken's place. A battered sofa, a couple of chairs and a scuffed guitar which he never plays on account of it being Margot's. Two huge bookshelves, stretching from floor to ceiling, half full of paperback novels, all of them dog-eared with broken spines. He'd read just about anything as long as it was cheap. Now that he's alone Bracken still needs something to while away the dark nights.

He loves those girls, but losing their mother broke things in him that won't ever heal. It was better that they went to live with his sister on her farm, across the river in New Jersey. It's a good place. Instead of a grimy city, they've got a life in the countryside surrounded by family, plus two cousins about their age. It's a better life. Better than watching their father die a little every day. Most of the money Bracken makes goes towards their future so they won't have to struggle like we did growing up.

"Thirsty work," said Bracken coming up the stairs. I noticed he was still wearing his thick work gloves. I passed him a beer and he drained half the bottle in three long gulps. "Honest work," he added.

Somehow he already knew that I was going to ask him to get involved with wasn't as clean cut as some of the jobs we'd done together in the past. "I didn't have any choice. One of Dolman's goons dragged me out of bed this morning."

Bracken raised an eyebrow. "Huh." It was practically a scream coming from him.

"I know. Karl fucking Dolman."

I laid it all out for him from the start with Caleb banging on my front door. When I'd finished we sat in silence for a while sipping our beers.

"How much are you paying?" he asked when his bottle was empty. I knew it wasn't greed. He'd walk into a fire for me without complaint. This was about providing for the girls after he was gone.

I peeled off a couple of notes and passed him the rest of the money I'd been given by Felix. Bracken flicked through the notes and grunted.

"How bad?" I asked, wanting to know what I was dealing with. Bracken said nothing for a while. We listened to the house creak around us. Eventually he pulled off his gloves, showing me the spread of the infection.

His right hand was unblemished. His left was criss-crossed with silver-grey threads that ran down his fingers, pooling on the tips and across his knuckles like congealed blood. There were also tendrils at the bottom of his palm, poised to creep up his arm. Dead flesh or even a blackened limb could be cut off, but this wasn't dead. It was just numb, inside and out. Blood still pumped and the fingers worked just fine. Not being able to feel if your hand was on the fire was only where it started.

Eventually, it would creep across his skin, encasing him in a cocoon of unfeeling flesh. The real danger was the damage I couldn't see. Because those grey threads were under the skin as well, changing Bracken's insides, and worse of all, they were in his head. Over time they'd erase his memories, eating away who he was. That was no way for anyone to live. Forgetting your own name was one thing. Forgetting the people you loved was something else entirely. Something horrific and unimaginable. I could understand why people with the Slate usually killed themselves.

"So far, nothing much has changed. I feel good. Normal," he admitted with a shrug. Bracken cocked his head to one side, waiting.

"Do you remember how we met?" I said, testing him.

"Your skinny ass was in trouble and I saved it. Like always."

"Good enough," I said, forcing a smile. It was difficult to know if he was hiding anything from me. Time would tell.

"Give me a minute. Finish your beer," said Bracken. He went out of the room and I heard him rummaging around in his wardrobe for some clean clothes. When he returned, he was dressed in a pair of black trousers, matching shirt and a leather jacket lined with wool. He'd swapped his work gloves for some tight leather ones that were moulded to his hands like a second skin. I kept my sword in plain sight on my hip to discourage trouble, but he didn't appear armed. Even though he probably wouldn't need it, I knew Bracken had a curved knife, practically a sword, tucked into the small of his back. It only came out in emergencies and when that happened, people got seriously hurt.

"Ready. So," said Bracken as we headed for the stairs, "what didn't you tell me?"

The question was reassuring, telling me that his mind was as sharp as ever. For now, at least.

"I've got some suspicions," I said. We both waved to the old crone downstairs as we passed but she said nothing, just gave me the evil eye.

As we headed back into the heart of Manhattan, I shared my ideas about what was going on. I had a horrible feeling that whatever happened, a lot of people were going to die. There was also the worrying thought that if Felix and his bumbling group of amateurs were already circling Dolman, searching for weaknesses, some of the bigger gangs were watching too.

My father had been a real son of a bitch. A mean drunk. Wore a big old ring on his right hand that tore a few chunks out of me over the years. I didn't visit him when he got sick and I pissed on his grave when he was dead. But if there was one thing he taught me without knowing, it was about weakness.

Dolman was a scary bastard, no doubt about that, but only because people thought him untouchable. But if someone could get to his daughter, then what did say about him? If he couldn't protect his own flesh and blood, what about his business? Or the people who worked for him? And if that was true, why should they stay loyal?

The longer this went on, the more difficult it would become for him to unpick. His people might be tempted to join the competition, share secrets, and help take down the big man at the top. A war seemed inevitable unless we quickly found Selina. If she wasn't found alive, then Dolman's retribution would be swift and brutal. Heads would, literally, roll.

But that was in the future. That was a what if. Right now, he'd been made to look human instead of a bogeyman, and that meant he was vulnerable.

Dolman wasn't a sheep, but there were wolves at the door, and they were out for his blood.

CHAPTER 5

It was just after midday when we made it downtown. We ate at a little hole in the wall café I'd frequented when I'd been a cop. Thankfully, the owner didn't recognise me. Either I'd changed in the interim years, or back then he'd only seen the uniform. The food was still the same: fresh, tasty and most importantly, clean. I knew the chicken he served wasn't his neighbour's dog.

Now came the hard part of the job. Some things never changed, whether I was a cop or a PI: wearing out shoe leather and knocking on doors. And having them slammed in my face. All part of the job. The difference was that now I didn't have a boss, just a client, and most of the time I could choose who I worked for. Just not today.

We started with the club Booker had told me about. It was closed until early evening but after banging on the door for a while, someone answered. The owner was stressed, cleaning up a stinking pile of vomit from the night before, and would have slammed the door in our faces if not for the fact that she thought I was a cop. I didn't dissuade her of that assumption and subsequently learned that Selina often came and went, but the owner didn't know much about her. She didn't even know Selina's surname, which was the only interesting thing we learned.

We spent the next couple of hours caught in a similar loop. I discovered Selina liked to move around. She regularly tried out new gay bars and up-and-coming clubs, but she never stayed long enough to become a regular. It was almost like she was searching for something, or maybe she was just restless. At this point, I was guessing. I didn't know enough about her personality, but I was trying to build a picture in my mind.

Though weary, we tried yet another club. This one was called Vixen. I'd only knocked a couple times when the door was yanked open as if someone had been waiting on the other side. A massive, bald, angry man covered in tattoos squinted at us.

"What the fuck do you want?" he asked, blinking against the light. The inside of the club had only mood lighting, leaving it thick with shadows and gloom. I could see people moving in the background, setting things up for tonight.

"I'm looking for a girl."

"Wrong kind of club, pal. This place is just for women."

"Are you a woman?" asked Bracken.

The big man blinked a few times and then came out all the way. In proper daylight I could see scarring on his hands, around his eyes and there were old knife scars on his forearms. He was a real brawler and by the look on his face, not much of a charmer.

"What did you fucking say?" asked the thug, glaring at Bracken.

"We're looking for Selina," I said, trying to avoid bloodshed. "Selina Dolman."

The thug's head whipped around, ending his staring match with Bracken. His posture changed as he looked up and down the street. "Inside," he said, waving us in.

For a couple of seconds I was practically blind, it was so dark in the club. Moving carefully to avoid falling on my face, I shuffled towards the bar, only clipping a couple of tables with my hip on the way. The lanterns behind the bar were turned down but the mirrors and glass bottles reflected their glow, creating a kaleidoscope of colours. There was just enough light for me to navigate and find my way to a bar stool.

Young, attractive women dressed in tight, revealing leather outfits moved behind the bar with confidence. They were used to working in the gloom, but my eyes were still adjusting. A few of the bar staff gave me and Bracken curious glances, but they didn't stop to chat. I guess they had work to do before tonight.

The big man came over to the bar and pulled out a stool so he could sit between us with his back to the door. The metal screeched across the tiled floor, setting my teeth on edge, but no one reacted to the noise.

We turned on our barstools and waited. He was nervous. Sweaty, despite the cool temperature of the room. I saw his gaze drift across the sword on my hip but he didn't seem alarmed. He was probably carrying a few knives, better suited for close work in crowded rooms. The bar was empty but I suspected it would be a different story tonight. Someone of his size would have to squeeze between tables and he'd stand out like a sore thumb, which was the point.

"Who sent you?" he asked, not giving us his name.

"A friend of hers called Booker," I replied, testing how much he knew about Selina's life. The big man was still anxious so I leaned into it. "Mr Dolman is worried about his daughter. He went by her place and someone had turned it over, made a real mess."

"I don't know nothing about that. Who'd be stupid enough to rob her?" he asked. Bracken studied the room as the thug talked, absorbing details.

We operated like this. I talked and he listened. Afterwards, he'd tell me everything I'd missed because I was too focused on the conversation.

The waitresses drifted around us like industrious ghosts.

"Does she come to this club very often?"

"Yeah, yeah, every now and then," said the big man, rubbing his bald head, his fingertips rasping against the stubble. "She's not been in for a few days, though. Last time was maybe five days ago. Melody would know."

"Melody?"

"Selina always asks for Mel to serve her."

"Is she in today?" I asked, hoping for our first piece of luck.

"Yeah, I think so. Hang on," he said, disappearing into the back of the club.

While he was gone, I got my first good look at the place. Lots of cosy booths around the edges of the room. A dance floor off to one side, next to a stage set for a band. Musicians were always in demand because people loved to drink and dance. There was an impressive array of bottles behind the bar and plenty of solid, polished woodwork. The furniture wasn't cheap and apart from being hardwearing, it had been put together by someone with skill.

"A lot of money in here," said Bracken, echoing my thoughts. He knew good craftsmanship when he saw it.

"Yeah."

"You see his hands shake?" he asked, raising one eyebrow.

"I noticed."

The big man was afraid, but it wasn't Selina's name that had triggered it, or her old man. Something else had him distracted. It might be something personal and unrelated, but I don't believe in coincidences. A coincidence just means there's a connection you haven't found yet. With enough digging and enough time, answers would come.

The bouncer returned with a slight woman in tow. Melody was young, maybe nineteen at a push, and probably a quarter of my weight soaking wet. In the right clothing, she could easily pass for a boy. Narrow hips, flat chested. Only her face told a different story. Big dark eyes in a heart-shaped face, cheekbones that could cut glass and dark hair shaped into an elfin bob. Melody smiled as she approached us but it didn't reach her eyes. She was nervous but not intimidated. I admired her grit, walking into a situation without knowing what it was about. She didn't hesitate and wasn't scared.

Like the other waitresses in the club, she was showing off a lot of skin, but despite the hot-pants, knee-high leather boots and vest, she had long sleeves that covered both arms. Bracken had noticed as well but he said nothing, merely raised an eyebrow at me. We'd talk about it later.

"Hi," she said, taking the offered stool. She smiled up at the big man who went back to sitting by the front door. "Joe's nice. Very protective."

It was a weird thing to say but I let it slide. She'd obviously misunderstood why we were here. Dealing with Selina probably meant she was used to people with money and power throwing their weight around. Maybe they asked her for unpleasant favours. It could be why she wore long sleeves. To cover up the bruises. Either that or she had track marks.

"Tell me about Selina," I said, keeping it general to begin with.

Melody shrugged, conveying much without saying anything. "What do you want to know? She's rich, and she usually asks for me. So, she gets what she wants."

From her tone, being Selina's favourite was a burden she'd prefer not to have. "Does she throw her weight around?" I asked.

"Sometimes," was the vague reply.

"You ever think about leaving."

Melody hesitated before speaking then lowered her voice. "Yeah, but if I go somewhere else, there's no way I'd get the same kind of tips."

Selina's name carried a lot of weight. After all, we'd been allowed in the club after a single mention of her name. If Selina Dolman was frequenting this establishment then it would encourage others to do the same, and that was good business for Vixen.

The silence between the three of us stretched. Bracken was

at ease with it. He could go a whole day without speaking if he wanted. I tried to imitate his calm and not fidget despite feeling impatient. Melody sniffed, shuffled on her stool, played with one of her dozen earrings and eventually sighed.

"Selina always drinks the same thing," she finally said. "She stays for a couple of drinks, tips heavily, and then leaves. I don't even know why she asks for me. I think it's a power thing. I'm not her type."

"What is her type?" I asked.

"She always goes for leggy blondes or redheads. Big girls," said Melody, lifting one shoulder, confused by the unwanted attention. Selina's focus on her could have been an obsession, if not for something more obvious. A clue I'd seen this morning and had only just pieced together.

Melody reminded Selina of herself at that age.

The painting on the back of Booker's door wasn't his daughter. It was Selina when she's been Melody's age. Judging by the sketch Booker had given me of Selina, she's grown a bit since then. I'd put Selina's current age at around thirty.

"Have you seen Selina with anyone lately? Anyone regular?" I asked, not knowing what term people Melody's age used for dating. It seemed to change every week, so I'd given up trying to stay current.

"I've seen her with this redhead." There was something in Melody's voice. Regret. Maybe Selina had offered her something more than a decent tip and Melody had turned her down. Or maybe she was thinking about a lost love of her own. "Last few weeks they've come into the club and taken over one of the booths. I serve them drinks and they talk for a couple of hours, then hit the dance floor. Some nights they stay until we close, other times they leave early together."

"Has Selina done that kind of thing before? Spent a lot of time with one person?"

Melody shook her head. "Usually it's a one and done thing,

twice if they're keen to please her. Everyone knows who she is and how much money she's got. Some women will do anything for a taste of that life." Melody didn't approve but it barely showed. That was probably the reason Selina hadn't tossed her aside in favour of another waitress.

Bracken glanced at me and this time, he raised both eyebrows. We were thinking the same thing. A break in routine. That couldn't be good.

"Do you know her name? The redhead?"

"She calls herself Rose, but that's just her working name. I think it's something boring like Jane, or Janet."

"Working name?" I asked.

"She's an expensive hooker. Only deals with women. There are a few like her around. They frequent all the girls' clubs looking for business," said Melody. "When it started with Selina, I thought it was just a business thing, you know? But then they came in together a second time, and then a third. They're always all over each other, so who knows?"

A hooker with a heart of gold who fell in love with one of her clients. Smelled like bullshit to me. It wasn't true love, so maybe it was just business. Selina had the money and from the sound of it, Rose had the looks. Women, and men, would throw themselves at Selina just to be near her. Power and money were powerful aphrodisiacs. It must have been strange for Selina to have someone refuse her advances, unless she paid for it.

"Are we done? I need to get back to work," said Melody. The other waitresses had continued working while we talked. She was getting a few looks for sitting still for so long.

"Last question. When did you last see Selina in here?"

"Five, maybe six nights ago. She was with Rose all night and they left together."

"Thanks for your help, Melody." I gave her a real smile but it had no effect. Either she couldn't tell if someone was being genuine or she just didn't care.

As she slid off the stool, Melody started rubbing her arms as if cold. One of the sleeves shifted, revealing dozens of tiny scars on her forearm, like tally marks. I'd seen wounds like that before. Melody caught me looking and quickly pulled down her sleeve in embarrassment.

Working in the club, night after night, where she pretended to be friendly, had taken a toll on Melody, numbing her in ways she'd not anticipated. That was my best guess, anyway. She worked in a club because she needed money to live, and she stayed at Vixen because her boss paid her extra to keep Selina happy. She was trapped and felt powerless. Cutting her flesh was Melody's attempt to regain some control over her own body.

I thanked Joe for his help and was glad to put the club behind us.

The weak afternoon sunlight stabbed at my eyes and it took a few minutes for them to adjust. As the city came back into focus, bringing with it a variety of unpleasant smells, I was reminded again why I lived in the suburbs. New York was a shithole that dragged you down, turning innocence into vice, preying on the weak, squeezing people for every drop of money and hope until they were lifeless, soulless shells.

The first settlers would be ashamed of what we'd become. Not because we'd shunned their technology and chosen to live relatively simple lives. It was far worse than that. We'd been given a fresh start unlike any other in history. The sins of the Old Country were so far away, I couldn't even fathom the distance in light years.

World wars. Bombs dropped from the sky that could wipe out an entire city in the blink of an eye. Poisoning the land for profit until it couldn't sustain life. Those hateful things were gone, and we weren't about to bring them back. We'd come so far, and yet other sins from the past were still with us in the present. Superstition. Racism. Prejudice and violence, worse than any animal, because the brutality was pre-meditated.

I shouldn't be here, caught up in some rich bastard's game of cat and mouse with his criminal rivals. I wanted to just go home, pick up a good book, and ignore all of it. I wanted not to give a shit. To pretend that whatever happened had nothing to do with me. But doing nothing made me culpable because I knew what was coming. Never mind what would happen to my health once Dolman found out I was trying to sit it out. Innocent people would get hurt, murdered, or caught up in it and have their lives bent out of shape. People like Melody. I wondered what she'd been like before being made into Selina's servant.

"You're brooding," said Bracken, wise to my moods after so many years.

"I'm pissed off. We shouldn't be here, caught up in Dolman's game."

"Yeah, but we are. Maybe, this way, we can help some people."

"I'm going to need something a bit more rousing than that, buddy. Give me a reason to keep going with this."

Bracken nodded, folded his arms, and leaned against a wall. "Do you know much about my people, from the Old Country?"

"Only what you've told me."

Over the years he'd shared bits and pieces, but I knew he'd done a lot of reading about his heritage. Most people were focused on the now, trying to work out who we are, but Bracken looked to the past to help him find his way forward.

"Many years ago, there was a great general. A white man's soldier. He fought hard for his people in a great war, although many now call him a coward. He slaughtered many from my ancestors' tribe and several others."

"I've gotta admit, I'm not feeling inspired," I said, but

Bracken ignored my interruption, as he often did. He rarely spoke at length about anything, but once he got started, there wasn't much that could stop him until he was done.

"The war was about freedom, but really it was about land and the white man's greed. The general was unstoppable, a man apart, and the future was bleak for my people. There was nothing ahead for us, only darkness. But then, the Great Bull had a vision of victory." Bracken's eyes widened as he stared at the sky, looking beyond the stars, looking back into history, to a time long before the first settlers were born.

"It inspired the tribes to unite, and soon after, there was a great victory. The general was killed, the men around him cut down like the grass against the scythe. The impossible became reality."

Bits and pieces of the story were vaguely familiar, either from school or stories he'd told me. Bracken bowed his head and gave me an expectant look.

"You're saying Dolman is like the general. That he can be beaten."

"No," he said, making an angry cutting motion with his hand. "You think in straight lines, Cole. Look deeper."

It was how I'd been trained as a cop. Follow the clues, piece together the evidence and build a picture, but this was outside my usual purview. It took me a while to see what he was getting at.

"Nothing is inevitable," I said. "Not even the future of this city." The Architects had been certain that this would become a steel and glass metropolis, like those found in the Old Country, and now against all the odds, the people had rejected the idea.

Bracken was right. I'd spent so long mired in the darkness of the city, trying to make sense of the worst cases, that I couldn't see the light. Although I'd not been a cop in years, my current gig still exposed me to the worst of humanity. Perhaps if I'd been a farmer or a craftsman, my worldview would be different. There were a lot of good people in the city, trying to do their best for themselves and their families. The only time I saw someone like that was when they had a problem that needed fixing.

The truth was, I didn't know what Selina's role was in all of this. Apart from being a spoiled rich kid, was she an innocent bystander in someone else's game, or was she a player? Up to now I'd been assuming the worst because of her family and how she'd been raised. I needed to shed my preconceptions and move forward with my eyes open. As Bracken said, I needed to stop thinking in straight lines.

"What did you think of Melody?" I asked, trying to distract myself.

"Bruised," said Bracken, which about summed it up. "Melody has lost all hope, but you haven't."

I wanted to argue with that but deep down, I knew he was right. Otherwise I wouldn't be here trying to find a missing girl. I'd be sat in bar somewhere, drowning my sorrows, numbing myself to the world, happily ignorant of others in pain.

In spite of all the shit that I'd gone through as a child, all of the brutality and misery I'd witnessed as an adult, somehow, deep down, I still believed there was good worth fighting for. Some stubborn, irritating part of me refused to give up, and it thought that all of us could be better.

"All right, let's go and find ourselves a hooker," I said.

CHAPTER 6

There are parts of New York I've visited regularly over the years because of my job as a cop, and sadly, the red-light district is one of them. I've not walked the streets often enough to be recognised, but I still know my way around.

This part of the city is not a place you stumble upon by accident. Five steps in and a tourist would turn around and quickly walk away because the intent is obvious. Huge provocative signs make it clear what's on offer. On my left there's a ten foot painting of a naked woman with massive bare breasts. Time and the weather have taken their toll, making her once-smooth features craggy and lined. The make-up is smudged, the smile is slipping and one of her teeth is missing. On my right the semi-naked man is faring no better. The peeling paint means the end of his cock is missing, and something is nesting in one of his eye sockets. I've rarely seen such grisly and yet accurate advertising for an area of the city.

The buildings are worn, draughty two-storey blocks made from old clay-fired bricks, metal roofs and plywood doors. Most of the windows have been replaced with wooden shutters, because glass is expensive if you have to replace it every week. Also, a shard of glass can be readily used as a dangerous weapon, and there's already enough risk without creating more problems.

Sex and crime seem to go hand in hand. Whether it's because of lust, jealousy, greed, envy or any of the other deadly sins, sex seems to get mixed up in just about everything. I've seen bodies mutilated, drowned, burned and ripped apart, and somewhere in that story, sex was always involved.

Personally, I don't care about your kinks. Whether you like to dress in leather and bark like a dog, get ridden by your girlfriend with a strap-on, or do it in the dark wearing nothing but blindfolds and slippers. Whatever turns you on. As long as it's not hurting anyone, unless they're also into that kind of thing.

Sex, when it's done right, is just about the best damn thing two people can do together. The kind of sex available on the streets is something else. Often it's connected to a world of pain, and very little of it is intentional.

As Bracken and I headed into the area, the haunted eyes of the walkers watched us for signs of danger. They were wary, and rightly so. Predators see them as vulnerable and easy prey. Besides, no one kicks up a fuss when one of them goes missing or turns up dead with their throat slit.

Many of the walkers were gaunt men and women, with skin that's too tight, eyes too large and not enough make-up to cover up a multitude of sins committed against their flesh. Burns, scars, track marks and discoloured tissue from communicable and nasty diseases. The exposed skin, an advert of what's available, doesn't tantalise or tease. It elicits sympathy and pity, but I make sure none of it shows. That's the last thing they want and it's likely to trigger a violent and vocal reaction.

I'm not here to judge or save them. It's not my job, and it's not one that I would ever want either. That's something for those who are better people than me. Those who care more deeply about others. My job comes later, typically once the flesh grows cold. That's where I can make the most difference. That's how I can help those left behind come to terms with who's been taken.

From a distance, the working boys already knew we were not interested in them, so they ignored us. Maybe it was the way we walked or our clothing, but the women began to swarm around us like brightly coloured butterflies. Their make-up and clothing created a façade of beauty, but those standing on the streets are low on the pecking order. I suspected Selina's special friend, Rose, had a somewhat more polished appearance and charged a lot of money for an hour of her time. She was also likely to have her own place in a nicer part of the district and was someone who was only available by appointment.

The offers made to us by the women would make most men blush or cause an instant hard-on. I'm sad to say that I'd heard it all before, so it had no effect, and Bracken showed all the emotion of a rock. When we failed to respond, the comments turned nasty but we kept walking, heading deeper into the seedy underbelly.

It was late in the afternoon and an annoying drizzle began to fall from the grey sky overhead. Despite lifting my collar, it trickled down the back of my neck, stuck to my skin, and left it feeling clammy and unwashed. Bracken said nothing but I saw him flex his hands as if he was expecting trouble. This area was dangerous. Some people wander in and never come out again. The walkers aren't without their own code and some of them have protection to keep them safe from those who try to take advantage.

A massive fleshy woman dressed in leather, carrying a long, curved sword, loomed out of the shadows. Her hair was scraped down to the scalp and her cold blue eyes were terrifying. A nasty scar split her bottom lip in two and there was a chunk missing from her chin. It looked as if someone took an axe to her face and barely missed. She was big, but moved with grace that told me she knew how to fight.

"Are you boys looking for company, or are you lost?" she asked in a surprisingly gentle voice.

"Neither. We're here on business. I'm looking for someone called Rose. Tall, redhead. Only caters to women."

"You a cop?"

"Something like that," I said, giving her a smile. The big woman grunted and put away her sword before walking forward. The closer she got, the more impressive she became, looming over both of us, making me feel like a child. She must have been nearly seven foot tall and four times my weight.

There was a harsh rawness to her features. She was someone who had seen it all before and it had taken a hefty toll. I doubted anything but the truth would work, and even then, it would be her decision to let us proceed.

"I'm Cole."

"Gert," she said which made Bracken twitch.

"That's my daughter's name," said Bracken sharing a rare smile with Gert. The big woman looked at him with suspicion, thinking he might be making fun of her. Slowly, she realised Bracken was being honest and her eyes softened.

"She's trouble, that one," said Gert, turning back to me. "Rose only caters to those with a lot of money, and she doesn't look after anyone but herself."

There are no guilds for prostitutes, and crimes involving them are a low priority for the cops. So whenever they can, they look after one another. It's a tough business and the only real friends they have, the only people who understand, are those living the same kind of life. It wasn't a smart move for Rose to turn away from the community and ostracise herself. It would leave her vulnerable and without loyal allies she could turn to in her hour of need.

"Is she the kind of person who would rip someone off?" I asked.

Gert nodded. "She's ruthless and greedy. Plus, she'd sell her own mother's snatch for a few coins."

"Can you tell us where to find her?" I asked.

At first, Gert said nothing. Instead, she looked me up and down and then shifted to Bracken, who met her gaze. I didn't know what she was looking for, but a person in her position had to be an excellent judge of character. Gert was far more adept than me at reading people and assessing how dangerous they could be. Risk versus reward was a daily part of her business. "You're an odd pair," she murmured. "I bet you've never come here for pleasure, right?"

"No," I said, knowing that Bracken would also never consider it. After Margot, there was no one else for him. As for me, it just wasn't a priority. I still had urges, no one had cut anything off, but these days, it seemed like a lot of effort. I'd rather spend the time alone with a drink and a good book.

"Rose lives on Melbrook," said Gert, gesturing to her left. "Four streets down, third on the right. She's in a ground floor apartment, so she might rabbit when you knock, but it's hard to know."

"Thank you," I said, offering Gert my hand. She looked at it for a moment before shaking it and then Bracken's hand. If a simple handshake was enough to surprise her, it made me wonder about the last time anyone had shown her genuine kindness.

Following Gert's directions, we headed for Rose's apartment. Almost immediately the buildings around us began to improve. The rusted metal roofs were replaced with tiles. The facades were clean, painted and all of the windows had glass in them. There were even a few colourful flower boxes and plants outside the front doors making them look homey.

No one was selling themselves on the street but at regular intervals I could see thugs lurking in the shadows of doorways or the lobbies of apartment buildings. Without an appointment, payment up front, and a promise of good behaviour, no one got past them. From the look of the few bruisers I saw, I knew they weren't idiots. They had the cool demeanour and precision of those with training. Former cops or soldiers. They watched us pass and didn't call out. Like Bracken, they would speak only when they had something to say.

Rose's building didn't have any muscle lurking outside, but the front door to the three storey apartment block was metal and there were two well-built locks. Six bell pulls, attached to metal chains, hung to one side of the door and a name had been painted on each. Someone had spent a lot of money on the building to ensure privacy and independence for its inhabitants. I suspected the other five apartments were also occupied by high-end hookers, but I was in no rush to find out.

"Shall I cover the back?" asked Bracken.

I considered it shook my head. "No, but keep an eye on her. If she's as good as I suspect, I could be in trouble."

People like Rose, or whatever her real name was, are dangerous chameleons. She didn't charge fifty times more than the streetwalkers for an hour because her pussy was magical. Clients were paying for everything that came with it. Without even seeing her, I knew Rose would be attractive, far above average, but that was only part of it. The experts could become whoever and whatever the client needed, almost at will.

With just a look, a pro could read a person's innermost desires and their personality would transform to match. Their every move, every touch, and even how they spoke became an act, perfectly adapted to please the client. It was an art.

I know my limits. I'm immune to erotic talk and dirty promises, but someone like her could turn my head and muddle my thoughts. She could play me for a fool and I wouldn't even know it. She might even send me off in a new direction with the investigation, and I wouldn't realise for days. By which time she'd be long gone and I'd be back to square one, feeling like an idiot with blue balls.

"I'll keep you grounded," promised Bracken, seeing that I was worried. I took a deep breath before calling on Rose. I pulled the chain twice but couldn't hear it ringing inside the building.

A short time later the front door opened slowly to reveal a gorgeous woman with flowing red hair and flawless creamy skin. She was dressed in a silk robe that covered most of her body, but it also managed to give me tantalising glimpses of her breasts and long legs. She was wearing little, or possibly no make-up, and was still more beautiful than any of the other hookers we'd seen. Her green eyes were wary, intelligent, and utterly dispassionate. I'd met sociopaths with more empathy.

"Rose?" I asked, somehow managing to swallow the lump in my throat.

"I only work with girls," she said, starting to close the door. "And I'm not interested in hiring a manager or muscle."

"We're here about Selina," I called, just as the door was closing. For a few seconds, all I could see was her perfectly manicured nails, but then the door opened wide. She studied us both, frowned at Bracken, probably because she couldn't get a read off him, then turned her attention to me. Warmth and colour seemed to flood her eyes and suddenly I was staring at a completely different person. I bit the inside of my mouth until I tasted blood. The stab of pain kept me focused.

"You should come inside," she said. Her movements were graceful as a dancer, and yet somehow her robe slipped open. I caught a brief glimpse of her colourful underwear before she pulled the robe tight. It wasn't accidental and yet I couldn't help staring. Knowing that she was trying to manipulate me didn't mean that I was immune. I realised I was fussing with my clothes as we entered her apartment, brushing away bits of dirt, trying to straighten my collar, and forced myself to stop. I didn't need to impress her and still found myself unconsciously trying. I was in trouble.

The front room of her apartment was remarkably ordinary with pastel walls, comfy and modest furniture with lots of fluffy cushions, and a bookshelf full of worn paperbacks. There were at least half a dozen plants in little ceramic pots and on the coffee table a mug of tea and her current read. From the picture on the cover, showing a semi-naked man riding a horse, I guessed it was a steamy romance. The door to her bedroom was slightly ajar but she pulled it closed before I could see what—or who—was inside.

Rose gestured us both towards the sofa and sat opposite in a large chair. With her hands delicately balanced on the armrests she made it resemble a throne. It felt as though we were two lowly supplicants coming to her for a favour. The notion wouldn't leave my head, and Rose gave me a wry smile as if she knew what I was thinking. But that was just my imagination—and libido—talking. There was no such thing as a mind-reader. Never had been.

Despite the fact that Rose had two large, armed men in her home, she was at ease. It was possible someone was lurking in the other room, ready to come to her defence if something went wrong, but I doubted it. She was supremely confident in her ability to control the situation, which was worrying. I had been hoping for a straight forward conversation.

"Tell us about Selina," said Bracken, taking the initiative, which was unusual but he could see I was distracted. Rose's smile slipped as she looked at him. A shadow passed across her face, her eyes darkened and her expression became haughty and cold. But when I blinked it was gone and I began to wonder if I'd imagined it. Her perfume was tantalisingly familiar. It was tugging at a memory, but I couldn't place it. It was floral.

"What would you like to know?" asked Rose, focusing on me. She was pretending that Bracken didn't exist and we were alone in the room, which was a bewildering and uncomfortable experience.

"Did someone hire you to befriend her?" he asked while I pulled the sleeves of my jacket straight. It was so rumpled it was just embarrassing. Rose untangled and re-crossed her legs while she pondered the question. I tried not to stare, took a deep breath and glanced at Bracken. His disappointment was like being doused with a bucket of cold water and I tried to pull myself together.

"Why do you ask?" said Rose, answering the question with one of her own. It was a technique I'd used many times, forcing the other person to reveal information without telling them anything. Then, depending on their answer, you could frame your response accordingly.

I folded my arms and sat back, gritting my teeth so I didn't say something stupid. We waited in silence as the seconds ticked away. Rose pursed her lips and her mask shifted again, becoming cool and reserved. She stopped playing with her hair and folded her arms across her chest.

"Did you actually care about her at all?" I wondered, sensing something beneath the surface. "Or was it an act?"

Rose shrugged. "We had fun and Selina was enthusiastic, but she's not my type," she added with a wink.

"Did you like her at all?" I asked. My question crinkled Rose's forehead and she sat forward, staring at me intently, a frown forming on her perfect lips.

"Why are you talking about her in the past tense?"

That answered one question. Either she wasn't complicit in whatever was going on, or she was a better actor than I realised. I'd have to ask Bracken if he thought she was telling the truth.

"Selina's been missing for two days," I said, deciding to share the reason for our visit.

Something that could have been concern passed across her face. "Missing? Do you mean dead?"

It was my turn to shrug. "Maybe. No one knows where she is. We know you were with her a few nights ago at the Vixen club."

"So what? We've been hanging out for weeks. I've not seen her in a few days, but she was fine when I left her." She sounded defensive and hurt, but I remembered what Gert had said. Rose cared only about herself.

"Did someone hire you to seduce her?" I asked. Rose sat back in her chair and folded her arms again.

"All we want to do is find her," said Bracken. "We don't care about the rest."

That wasn't strictly true, but right now I had the feeling if we received any useful information from this meeting then it would have been worthwhile. Who hired Rose would have to remain a mystery, unless we found someone else who could point us in the right direction. The most important thing was finding Selina, and hopefully that would be enough to prevent a gang war.

I thought about using empathy, posing what-if scenarios where Selina could be hurt if we waited too long, but I doubted it would have any effect. Rose was amazing at creating moods and simulating emotions, but I wondered if she was capable of having real ones anymore. Or, like Melody, had she become numb to the world?

"Tell us what happened," I said, not posing it as a question. I couldn't command her to do anything. It was all up to her. I didn't want to play games because I knew I'd probably lose.

"It's not a big thing," said Rose, playing it down but there was a hint of guilt in her voice. She may not have been told that something bad would happen to Selina but Rose wasn't stupid. I folded my arms and waited while Bracken remained motionless.

Rose rolled her eyes and some of the façade slipped away, revealing someone more annoyed than upset at our intrusion and the potential danger her actions posed to Selina.

"She's rich and entitled. Everyone clamours for her attention. I made her pay for it. It wasn't a difficult job."

There were faster and easier ways to make money. It seemed unlikely that someone was trying to exploit Selina, which brought me back to the other question. Why?

"So you befriend her, seduce her, and then what?" I asked.

"You want the details?" asked Rose, nibbling on one of her fingernails. I cleared my throat and shook my head, trying to focus. I knew she trying to manipulate me, set my imagination on fire, but it didn't stop my mind from creating erotic images. The raw sexual energy pouring off her was incredible and somehow her perfume was stronger than before. Was it jasmine?

"What was it for?" asked Bracken, cutting through the tension like a knife. "Why did they hire you? Blackmail?"

"Don't know. Don't care," said Rose, and it was probably the truest thing she'd said to us.

"A woman in your position must be able to charge a significant amount for your company. Engaging your services for weeks at a time would be expensive." It would probably have cost a small fortune, which begged the question again, why? What was the pay off?

"It paid well," said Rose, with an elegant shrug, although I thought she was being modest.

"So why did it end? Did she realise it was an act?" I asked.

"Don't be ridiculous," said Rose, spitting out the words. "She had no idea."

I didn't think it would be that easy to get under her skin but Rose took pride in her abilities to deceive and manipulate others. Everyone has an Achilles heel and it seemed like I'd just stumbled across hers. "Then what happened?"

"The job was done. We went out, got drunk, then I dropped her off and that was it."

"But you didn't take her home," I said, making an educated guess.

"No," said Rose. "I was told to take her somewhere."

We knew what that meant. This had been orchestrated so that Selina would trust Rose. Enough to lower her guard, allowing Rose to take her somewhere new without it arousing any suspicion. She'd probably told Selina it was going to be wonderful surprise and she'd gone willingly. At that point, someone must have grabbed Selina. They were probably holding her hostage.

The worst part was that Rose had a complete lack of remorse. Any lingering physical attraction I had for her was burned away in an instant. She was more grotesque than any of the desperate streetwalkers we'd seen earlier.

"Where?"

"She won't be there anymore," said Rose.

"You're probably right. In which case, it wouldn't hurt to tell me."

It was possible Rose wouldn't tell me out of spite, or because I'd insulted her talent. Nothing had changed since the moment we'd walked in. She was still in control. All I could do was wait.

"What's his story?" asked Rose, jerking a thumb at Bracken. He was probably one of only a handful of people she'd met that she couldn't read or manipulate. It must have been infuriating.

I shared a smile with my old friend and said "He's complicated."

"Fine," said Rose, tired of us both. She wrote down an address and slid the note across the table. "Get out."

All traces of the temptress were gone and what remained was something hollow, bitter and ugly. We wasted no time leaving her building and making our way out of the red-light district. By the time we'd put the street walkers a fair distance behind us I was feeling better. Against the odds, we had another clue and were one step closer to finding out what had happened to Selina. For once, the investigation was going smoothly.

As we rounded the next corner, I came face to face with Felix and five of his Warlords, all of them armed and pumped for a fight.

"What the fuck are you playing at?" asked Felix, waving a dagger in my face.

CHAPTER 7

"You'll have to be more specific," I told Felix, casting an eye over the youngsters he'd brought with him.

One was the girl with the broken nose and I could see that she was desperate for revenge. She and the others were armed with daggers, all of them itching for a fight. The beating I'd previously given them hadn't been enough. They still thought they were invulnerable and would live forever. I remember being that young and that stupid.

Apart from the odds, the most worrying thing was that there was no sign of Duke. Last time he'd been watching the fight a short distance away, armed with a crossbow. If this conversation went poorly—and it was already off to a bad start—I didn't want to get a bolt in the ribs for a snarky comment.

"I thought we had a deal," said Felix, who seemed genuinely shocked that I'd taken his money and then not done as we'd agreed. Then again, he was an idiotic thug playing at being a gangster, so it wasn't too surprising. "You were supposed to leave this alone. I paid you to take a holiday. Then what I do hear? You're asking questions about Selina fucking Dolman."

"Oh that," I said, scanning the rooftops and corners for any shadows that didn't belong. I couldn't see anyone but that didn't mean Duke wasn't there. "I just said that to get out of the warehouse. I didn't want to get shot by Duke. By the way, where is your boss?"

"I'm in charge," said Felix, brandishing his dagger, waving it around like an idiot. Bracken slowly moved to my left until I could see him in my peripheral vision. That side was covered, now I had to worry about something coming at me from my right or the front.

"Right, of course," I said, holding up my hands, in a mock surrender. "That's why you look to him before you do anything. Does he tell you when to wipe your arse?"

"You should watch your lip," said Felix. Behind him, the other Warlords were getting twitchy. They'd come here expecting a fight and so far all we'd done was talk. Their patience was wearing thin.

"This was your idea, right?" I said, gesturing at our location. "Duke wouldn't be that stupid. Attacking someone out in the open, when there are many ways to escape."

While they glanced around at the streets, I retrieved my punching dagger but kept it concealed inside my jacket.

"He was holding me back. Holding all of us back," said Felix, and his idiot companions mumbled in agreement. "So I relieved him of his money and then his life."

I didn't know Duke and had only met him the one time, but he'd been a lot more likeable than Felix and the rest of his cronies. He'd also had intelligence and the bearing of someone with experience and wisdom, two things which the Warlords lacked. I felt a twinge of disappointment that he was gone but also relief because it meant Felix had shown up without any backup.

"Walk away now and you get to live. If you stay, you'll be responsible for what happens to the rest of your crew," I said, readying myself. I already knew he wouldn't listen but I had to try. Sometimes people can surprise you and I hoped that this was one such occasion. I already had enough blood on my hands and knew all too well what it felt like to watch a friend die in front of me. "As the leader, you're responsible for them. Be smart about this."

Felix laughed, demonstrating his arrogance. "You're more stupid than you look. We outnumber you."

"This isn't a game," I said, hoping to get through to him. All but one of his followers were oblivious to the threat the two of us posed. Only the young red-head was alarmed and there was more than fear in his eyes. As he stared at Bracken the lad's hands began to shake. The others were nervous, almost bouncing on their toes with eagerness, but he was scared. Adrenaline and arrogance was roaring through their veins. Making them believe they would live forever and were unstoppable.

"Felix," said the redhead, but no one was listening.

"Last chance," I said, shifting my balance to my back foot.

"Kill them," said Felix.

A second later I punched him in the chest, straight through the heart. He dropped to the ground and I knew he would be dead in seconds. I'd felt the punching dagger go through his sternum. The wound was small and there wasn't much blood on his shirt.

The others didn't realise what had happened and charged, screaming bloody murder. The girl with the broken nose came at me, screeching like a banshee, desperate for payback. I broke one of her knees with the heel of my boot and opened a six-inch slice down her forearm with my dagger. She dropped to the road, bleeding and crying in pain.

Three Warlords ran at Bracken and he wasted no time dealing with them. He batted away a dagger with his right hand, and his left fist collided with the face of the first thug. The force was so great it shattered the kid's nose, broke his cheek and several teeth went spilling onto the ground, rattling like dice. The lad would be disfigured for life, if he survived.

Another jabbed her dagger at Bracken's side, but the point of the blade snapped as if it had been made of glass. Before she could react Bracken elbowed the girl in the face, dislocating her

NEW YORK MINUTE

jaw, and she spun away, already unconscious.

We had one more Warlord each and I'd been left with the nervous redhead. In a few seconds he'd witnessed his friends being dismantled. He still held a dagger in one hand, but had clearly forgotten about it. Bracken had his last opponent by the throat and was squeezing the lad's neck until he dropped his weapon and began to splutter, gasping for air.

"What's it going to be?" I asked the last Warlord. He didn't waste any time and threw down his dagger then took several steps back with his hands up. "Before you run, I want you to remember what you've seen here today." I said, hardening my voice. The lad being choked had turned bright red, his tongue protruding like a tired dog. His feet were off the ground and he flopped about like a fish on the riverbank.

"In the future, am I going to have a problem with the Warlords?" I asked.

"No, I promise," said the kid, whose voice had risen in pitch, indicating his real age was less than he pretended. His world had just been turned upside down. His friends were crippled and his boss was dead. The façade of being a hardened criminal gang had been erased, like a fart in the wind. The surge of adrenaline had left the boy jiggling like an addict desperate for a fix.

I could see that he was barely holding on. The girl at my feet was still screaming from the shattered knee and her cries had become strangled sobs. The redhead winced at the pitch of her voice and was ready to bolt.

"Get out of here," I said, and he ran, not pausing to see what happened to his friends. Bracken dropped the other kid, who fell to the ground and lay there gasping for air. I could see red marks on either side of kid's neck and knew there would be bruises.

Bracken's expression had barely changed but I could see that he was troubled. I shook my head, disappointed that we'd

69

been forced to do this, and I knew he shared my regret. Beating up a bunch of enthusiastic but unskilled idiots wasn't my idea of a good time.

We left them in the street and no one rushed to their aid. There was blood on my hands and more of it spattered on my clothes. I didn't like the way it felt and tried to scrub it off against my trousers. I walked in no particular direction, my enthusiasm about finally getting somewhere with the case derailed by the fight. Bracken said nothing. He remained at my side, a silent and reassuring presence. Someone else might have made a joke to try and lighten the mood, but he did neither. He knew me too well to try that. I also knew that he didn't blame me for what had happened to Felix and he wasn't judging me either.

Besides, he had own worries. I'd seen how hard he'd hit the first Warlord. It had practically taken the kid's head off. He was a man who had always been in control. Of his emotions, of his body and his mind. The city was continually teetering on the brink of chaos but Bracken didn't try to change it. He radiated calm and, in turn, others were affected by his presence. Wherever he went, he created change. I'm far less subtle in my methods. A fist in the face or a kick in the crotch is my go-to.

"How bad is it?" I said, gesturing at his side. The only reason for a knife to break like that was that either because Bracken was wearing some kind of body armour under his clothing, or it was the Slate.

"Not too bad."

"Should I be worried?" I asked, not wanting to nag, but I was worried. Also, selfish as it was, I needed him for this case and I couldn't do it without him. I'd already killed one person today and my gut told me that, however this ended, more blood would be spilled. Hopefully none of it would be mine.

"Not about me," said Bracken, gesturing at a local café. We went inside and I rinsed my hands in the bathroom while he ordered some drinks. The waitress brought two mugs of steaming coffee and two slices of apple pie. My hand rattled against the cup and I took a moment to steady myself before trying for another sip. I ate a mouthful of pie, needing the sugar to settle my jangling nerves.

I told myself that Felix had it coming. That he deserved it, but I hadn't done it because he'd killed Duke, or the poor guy in the warehouse. I'd done it because I wanted to. I had given him a warning, he hadn't listened, so it was his fault. Except that was also a lie. I could have just injured him like the others. Instead, I'd punched him in the chest, knowing he didn't stand a chance and that it would kill him.

The truth was that it had been easy to kill him. Far too easy.

He wasn't my first but it had been a while.

"A young man like that, always looking for trouble, sooner or later it would've found him," said Bracken, around a mouthful of food. "Mm, good pie."

"So it's not my fault. Is that what you're saying?"

Bracken shrugged. "Do you think it's your fault?"

A simple question from him was never just that. He was always asking something else as well. You just had to look deeper.

The whole gang had always been heading for trouble. So far only Duke, and now Felix, had died. Some of the others were injured but they still had their lives. How long that continued really depended on them.

The first beating hadn't got through to them, despite how easily I'd taken them down by myself. It had only bruised their pride, not changed their minds. My hope was that this fight would be enough to scare them straight and set them on a new path. The redhead would never become a part of the underworld. I knew that for sure, but I was less certain about the others. Either they'd come for me again, and we'd have to deal with them, or the Warlords were through.

"It would have happened eventually. I just wish it hadn't been me," I said, thinking about what I should have done differently while I ate my pie and drank coffee.

When I was done Bracken tapped the table. "Enough. We must move forward. You can tear yourself apart another day."

"Right. Let's go."

It was very likely the address Rose had given us would be abandoned, but there might be clues, or even better, a witness to what had happened. Once Selina realised that Rose had led her into a trap, she would have fought back, maybe caused a ruckus, and hopefully someone had seen or heard something.

The afternoon was getting on, evening approached and there were streaks of black running through the sky. This would have to be our last call today, but for once, the timing was perfect. This time of night brought out a different crowd of people. The workers went home and the night crowd filled the streets and dark corners. If Selina had been snatched late at night, there was a chance one of them would have seen something.

We were just crossing a wide avenue that was fairly busy with people when I noticed we were being followed. A chubby balding man dressed in a long grey coat was keeping pace with us. I saw his reflection in a shop window and a few minutes later, after several turns, he was still there. He maintained the same distance and was doing his best not to appear interested in us, but his intent was clear.

I wasn't sure how long he'd been following us but I hadn't seen anyone in the red-light district. My guess was he had simply waited for us to re-emerge and had then picked up our trail again. If my assumption was true, that meant he'd witnessed the fight with the Warlords and had done nothing to intervene. It also meant there was more than one watcher as there were numerous ways in and out of the district. If he was working alone there was no way he could have picked up our trail so quickly.

It took me a little while, because they weren't amateurs, but eventually I spotted a second shadow. The hawk-faced woman was on my far left and a little while later, I found the third, a fresh-faced lad who barely looked out of his teen years. Although none of them were dressed the same, they were definitely working together. Even more disturbing was a notion that I knew the man following us.

As I turned to Bracken and was about to raise my concern he nodded. "I know." His eyes slid to the right and then the left. I tilted my head back slightly, indicating someone behind and Bracken frowned, irritated that he hadn't noticed the third person following us. At first I thought they were trying to box us in, but all of them were maintaining their distance. We would need a distraction to escape their notice.

Most of the people around us were hurrying home from work but there was a growing number getting ready for a night out. I spotted a couple of scantily dressed working girls grab a drink at a table outside a café, loading up on caffeine for the long night ahead. A trio of burly men, probably bouncers for a bar, were swapping stories while stuffing their faces with questionable meat kebabs from a street vendor. An old-fashioned pub had opened early and from inside, I could hear the faint wheeze of someone's singing accompanied by an out of tune piano. The gaggle of twenty-somethings drinking outside on the street were only interested in the alcohol, not the ambience, but they could still be useful.

As we came abreast of them I nudged the elbow of one girl who spilled her drink over someone else. Bracken and I kept moving as an argument started behind us, voices rose in volume and blame started being thrown around. I headed inside the pub, taking us off the street and out of sight before one of the drinkers realised we had been responsible.

The woman half asleep behind the bar started to lift herself off her stool but I waved at her to stay put. We walked through the common room, down to the toilets and out the back door to the alley behind. Picking up the pace, we jogged east and then south along grimy alleyways, cut back on ourselves, going west along quiet streets, and then carried on south.

Both of us had been looking since we left the pub and neither Bracken nor I had caught sight of anyone following us. I was confident that we'd thrown off our shadows when we rounded a corner and found two of them waiting for us in the middle of the street, the woman and the new recruit.

"Cole Blackstone. Someone would like a word with you," said the hawk-faced woman, opening her coat to reveal her tin badge. In the old days, long before I was born, and long before I'd put on the uniform, cops had carried silver badges. The problem was that pickpockets kept stealing them and melting them down, so they'd downgraded it to something almost worthless.

I didn't need to read the lettering on her badge to know what it said. I had carried an identical one for years. The new recruit took out his badge as well and held it up like a shield in front of him. The woman beside him rolled her eyes but said nothing. In addition to a severe face, her eyes were cold and her hair scraped back in a ponytail so tight that it looked like it hurt.

"Let's not make a scene," said the chubby guy, stepping out from behind us. He was accompanied by four constables in grey uniforms, all of them young and well-built. Two of them had visible scars on their faces, indicating that they'd already seen a fair bit of action on the streets of New York. All of them were armed with swords but each had a steel baton held at the ready in one hand. They were grim-faced and silent, smart enough not to take anything for granted, despite the odds. Two of them were eyeing up Bracken, who hadn't reacted.

"Come on, Cole, it's just a chat," said the older guy, taking a step forward. The woman, clearly the one in charge, frowned at his familiarity.

"Do I know you?"

"A little. Name's Michael O'Neill. I was coming up when you were heading out the door." I vaguely remembered him, had probably only met him twice in passing, but I never forgot a face.

"Shut it, O'Neill," said the woman, reasserting her authority. "Last chance, Cole."

If someone wanted to talk to me, there were a number of ways that were easier. Turning up with so many bodies seemed heavy-handed. They were obviously expecting trouble, but I didn't know why. My reputation wasn't that bad. The woman was staring at me with something bordering on hate, as if I'd personally betrayed her.

Seconds ticked by. The uniforms started to sweat, their knuckles turning white on their batons.

Bracken glanced at me and raised an eyebrow. We'd faced similar odds a couple of hours earlier and had escaped unscathed, but this was different. They weren't bumbling amateurs and had been able to track me across the city, which was impressive. Despite my admiration for their abilities, I didn't like being strong-armed by anyone, cop or criminal.

If we fought them it would be bloody and brutal. Besides, someone only wanted to speak with me. There was no need for me to put Bracken in danger again.

"Our last stop of the night will have to wait," I said, gesturing for Bracken to stand down.

O'Neill heaved a sigh of relief and waved the uniforms back. Hawk-face walked forward until we were almost nose to nose. She had to tilt her head to look up at me and I think that burned her the most.

"Do we know each other?" I asked.

"Gods no," she said, as if I was something stuck to the bottom of her shoe. "Let's go."

Hawk-face gave Bracken one final look and, much to my surprise, he smiled. She stumbled and would have fallen if not for her colleague who caught her by the elbow. Once she was steady on her feet, she yanked her arm away and marched ahead of everyone.

"Oh shit," said O'Neill, under his breath. "It's going to be one of those nights."

It certainly was.

CHAPTER 8

With O'Neill walking beside me, and two constables in uniform behind, I could almost pretend I was a cop again and they were part of my squad. The illusion was spoiled by Hawk-face and her protégé in front. Beyond them were the other two constables, clearing the way and keeping an eye out for trouble.

"What's her deal?" I whispered to O'Neill. "She looks at me like I just pissed on her shoes."

He winced but didn't have a chance to answer. As if she knew we were talking about her, Hawk-face glared over her shoulder. I smiled and waved until she turned away with a sneer.

"Can you at least tell me their names?" I asked.

O'Neill considered it for a moment. "She's Rivera and the greenhorn is Dallas."

"No talking!" snapped Rivera, who seemed intent on taking the fun out of everything.

Even before I started recognising some of the streets, I knew where they were taking me. It was an ugly building, made of thick grey stone where the windows were narrow, lined with steel bars and the metal doors were reinforced. The roof was steep, edged with metal spikes and I knew there were also three hatches inside for easy access. If there was ever a siege, this was the place to be. Once the doors were closed, and the metal shutters bolted from the inside, it became an impenetrable fortress. It was also the same building where I'd worked for many long and difficult years, before leaving to become a private investigator.

The central headquarters of the New York police department. What a shithole. Long before I left the Force, I'd come to loathe the building because of what it represented. It wasn't the people, although some of them were hideous, and it wasn't the work. It was the system.

Like many others, I'd joined with noble intentions, bright eyes and a can-do attitude. I'd been determined to clean up the city, bring criminals to justice, and help my fellow humans. What I hadn't realised, and what quickly became apparent, was that the police were a clean-up service. We weren't there to prevent crimes, just solve them. The police always investigated after the fact. We waited until the body was cold, the robbery was done, the building burned down and the ashes were cool.

It could have been different, but it wasn't my problem anymore. I'd left the police, and all of its internal politics and bureaucracy, behind me. Or so I'd thought. And yet here I was, being marched up to the front door like a criminal.

A single blue-panelled lantern hung outside the front door. A tiny dot of light that told people where to go when they wanted to report a crime. Rivera rapped her fist on the door and a few seconds later, a slot opened at eye level.

"Let me in," she said, not bothering to identify herself, which I knew was a breach of protocol. Even if you knew the person at the door, even if they were your best friend in the world, you were supposed to state your full name and the daily safe word. It was a security precaution in case someone was there under duress. Without the password, the door would stay shut. I was surprised to hear the scraping of heavy bolts. It seemed that security had become lax since my last visit to police headquarters.

The tight corridors were unchanged. The walls were bare and the building had the same unpleasant smell I remembered, a mix of stale sweat, old blood, and musty paper. The ground floor was purely reserved for scribes and other admin people who required the most natural light. There were always reports to write, witness statements to take down and old files to copy as the ink faded. At this hour the rooms were awash with bright yellow light spilling out from specially made oil lamps. In the day mirrors reflected sunlight into each room, making them exceptionally bright and warm. With so much critical paper lying around, the cops of the past had learned the hard way about evidence and statements, literally, going up in smoke. Candles were banned from the building and there hadn't been a fire in decades. The oil lamps were almost indestructible. You could drop one on the floor and it wouldn't break.

Rooms on either side of the corridor were busy with people in uniform and civilians crying, begging for justice or sitting in stony silence. Many had blank expressions and had been rendered mute by the shock of their brutal experiences. Sadly I'd seen the same expression many times.

I followed Rivera and the greenhorn, Dallas, down several flights of worn steps into the earth. O'Neill trailed behind me, dragging his feet. We stopped three levels underground, a floor typically used for interviewing suspects. To my surprise, I was escorted to an office at the end of the hall. Mirrors and clever channels dug into the ground normally filtered sunlight into the room, but tonight it was lit only with two lanterns fixed to the back wall.

The only furniture in the room was a scuffed desk, two chairs and a stack of papers in neatly labelled folders.

With such weak lighting, shadows pooled in the corners of the room. Rivera went to stand in one and Dallas the other. O'Neill lurked by the door, waiting for something. The click of heavy boots announced a new arrival and I knew their identity long before I saw his face. No one else had a steel plate fitted to the base of his right boot. Thump, click. Thump, click.

"Thanks for coming in," said Chief Langley, taking a seat

behind the desk. With a wave, he dismissed O'Neill, who closed the door with him on the other side.

Walter Langley had been born with one leg slightly shorter than the other, and had been labelled a cripple by the doctor. His mother was also told that he was slow in the head and wouldn't amount to much. He'd certainly pissed all over that prediction, rising to become Chief Constable. Somewhere in his late fifties or early sixties, Langley was a short man with a weak chin and grey hair. You wouldn't look at him twice as, physically, he was unremarkable. It was only his green eyes that told a different story. He'd grown a goatee since last I'd seen him, and it hadn't improved his ferret-like face.

"As if I had a choice," I said, gesturing at Rivera. "Why so heavy handed?"

"Inspector Rivera thought you would resist my invitation. I thought it wiser to err on the side of caution."

"So, you've got me here. Why?" I heard muttering from the corner of the room. "Something you'd like to share, Rivera?" I asked.

"Are you going to let him talk to you like that, Sir?" she said, ignoring me.

"Cole and I are old friends," replied the chief.

"I wouldn't say that," I said. "I remember telling you to 'fuck off and die' the last time we were face to face." The greenhorn gasped but Langley just chuckled.

"Scum," spat Rivera.

"What's her problem?" I asked.

"Oh, Rivera doesn't like you, because you used to be one of us and now you work for criminals," said the chief.

"Unfortunately, now that I'm an independent investigator, I don't have my fellow officers to watch my back. That means I don't always get to choose my clients. Sometimes, I go where I'm told. I'm often at the whim of powerful arseholes." I knew it was a mistake to underestimate the chief, but that didn't mean

NEW YORK MINUTE

I was going to stop taking digs at him. No one rose to power, in any organisation, without being some kind of a bastard.

"Karl Dolman is a dangerous man," conceded the chief, assuming I was talking about someone else. "And it's tragic what's happened to his daughter. He must be worried."

There wasn't a hint of emotion in his voice. Looking around the room, it became obvious that I was the only one who actually cared about the fate of Selina Dolman, never mind the repercussions.

"Well, so far she's just missing. No one actually knows what's happened to her, right?" I waited, hoping that he wouldn't tell me her body was downstairs cooling on a stone slab.

"Of course, it's just speculation at this point," said Langley, waving a hand. I suspected he knew something, but there was no way to make him tell me. His mind was like an impenetrable steel trap. He could not be manipulated, blackmailed or bought. "I invited you here to tell you that Selina Dolman's disappearance has been officially labelled a kidnapping. As such, it now warrants an official police investigation."

"Really?" I said, playing along.

"Absolutely. She's the daughter of an important person in the city."

"Who you happen to despise," I pointed out.

"True, but we can't let something like this slide. It might create a dangerous precedent. The children of city officials might be kidnapped and ransomed. No, this cannot be allowed to stand."

I didn't believe Langley. Not for a second.

"Well, I was hired by the family, so until they tell me that my services are no longer required, I'm going to keep looking."

Langley pursed his lips and considered his next words carefully. I wondered if anything I'd said so far had actually surprised him in the slightest. Many years ago we had been good friends. I'd changed a lot since that time, what I now viewed as the bad old days.

"I could have Rivera lock you up in a cell until this is over," pointed out the chief.

"You could, but you won't," I said, sounding more confident than I felt.

"Really? And why is that?"

"Because you're a stickler for the law. Because you can quote it, chapter and verse, and because I've not committed any crimes."

"Not yet, but you could be obstructing an official police investigation."

I laughed at that. "We both know you won't get off your arse until it's over."

"Watch your mouth," snarled Rivera, but I ignored her.

Langley remained calm but he was studying me, searching for something. "This is too big for you, Cole. You're a one-man operation. You should walk away. After all, isn't that what you're good at?"

"You miserable old cunt," I said.

Part of me was tempted to reach across the desk and smash his teeth in, but I didn't, because that's exactly what he wanted. The chief loved manipulating people. He was good at it, too. Despite knowing all his tricks, he'd still managed to get under my skin. Hurting him would be the perfect excuse to lock me in a cell until this was over. Then there would be one less player for him to worry about.

Tension filled the room and I sensed his disappointment which made me grin.

"This is your one warning. Stay away," said Langley.

"I'll think about it," I said, knowing I would do no such thing.

The fact that I was in police headquarters, having this conversation with the chief constable, told me there was a lot more going on than I had realised.

He dismissed me with a flick of his hand. Dallas opened the door and I found O'Neill waiting in the hallway. The others stayed behind as he escorted me back upstairs to the surface. I wondered if the chief was still one step ahead of me. Had he known what I had done and planned for this outcome as well? It didn't matter.

I thanked O'Neill, mostly for being a decent human compared to the rest, and was glad to put the police station behind me. That was twice that I had been warned off this case. There was more going on than I knew but that didn't change the facts. I had to find Selina Dolman and do it fast. Otherwise, bloody murder would follow, possibly mine.

I trudged back to Bracken's house and found him on the front steps sipping a beer. There was no sign of Mrs Van der Berg and her front room was dark, so I guessed she'd already gone to bed. I followed Bracken upstairs. He passed me a beer and we sat in silence, taking a moment to relax and process everything.

It had been a long day and I'd covered a lot of ground since being woken up by Caleb. It was late and too far to consider travelling all the way home only to come back tomorrow morning, especially when Bracken had a spare room.

I told him about the meeting I'd just had with my old boss. As usual, he listened in silence and his face gave nothing away. I'd seen statues with more expression.

"So, what do you think?" I asked when I was done.

"Someone is lying," said Bracken.

It wasn't what I had expected him to say. Of course someone was lying, probably everyone we'd spoken with had been lying about something, but Bracken never wasted words.

"We're still missing something," I surmised. Someone, probably more than one person, was trying to steer us in the wrong direction.

"I'm too tired to figure it out tonight."

"The sheets are clean," he said, gesturing at the spare bedroom.

"Thanks," I said, heading for the promised bed, but then paused and turned back. "Are you not going to sleep?"

"In a bit. I'm going to sit up a spell."

"Can you still sleep?" I asked, worried about the Slate. There was still so much we didn't know about the long-term effects because most people with it gave up too quickly.

"I sleep fine. Just thinking," promised Bracken, giving me a rare smile.

I took him at his word and, after kicking off my boots and climbing between the sheets, was asleep in no time.

NEW YORK MINUTE

CHAPTER 9

The next morning we stopped at a local café for some breakfast. After eating a plate of fried sausages, bacon and eggs, washed down with two large cups of coffee, I felt awake and ready for the day. Even though I'd scrubbed my fingers, there was still blood under my nails. I tried not to dwell on it.

We needed answers and there were lots of ways to get them. The easiest way to loosen people up was the carrot, not the stick. I dropped Bracken off at another café and headed for the Squat Tower by myself. There was no need for Dolman to know that I was working with someone else and besides, I suspected the Warlords weren't the only ones watching the place.

After navigating the stairs, I reached the top with burning thighs and not much air left in my lungs. I'd timed it perfectly and today I didn't interrupt breakfast. Once I explained who I was to the guards at the door, and they'd frisked me several times, I was escorted inside. Dolman was still at the breakfast table in his dressing gown and slippers, smoking a cigar. Around him were half a dozen plates, a few scraps of food, and some crusts someone had refused to eat.

"That didn't take long," he said, waving the guards away.

"I haven't found her yet," I said, not wanting him to get the wrong impression.

"Then why are you here?" he asked, stubbing out his cigar on an expensive plate. It would probably leave a stain.

"I'm being stonewalled. People are scared to talk because

it's you." It wasn't a total lie. His name carried a lot of weight in the city and it had opened doors for me that might otherwise have remained shut, but it also made people nervous, which made things more difficult. There were numerous schemes and plans in mid-flow that I was getting caught up in just by being in proximity to Dolman. Being warned off by the Warlords and the police were two complications that wouldn't happen if it was anyone else.

"Don't you carry a sword?" he asked.

"Yes."

"Then use it to get some answers."

I took a breath before replying. He was not the kind of person who responded well to snarky comments. "That's not why you hired me. Besides, I'd rather not leave a trail of bodies. I'm trying to do this as discreetly as possible."

Dolman kept stubbing out his cigar even though it was definitely out. I could see the muscles jumping in his arm and the sides of his face. "You want me to pay you."

"I need to bribe some people."

I felt no sympathy. He knew the risks of being in his particular line of work. It was dangerous, but he'd accepted them because of the rewards. But it seemed as if, only now, Dolman was starting to realise the effect it had on those closest to him. If they didn't have them already, I suspected his youngest children would soon find themselves with bodyguards.

He finally left the cigar alone, gave me a long, unreadable look and then stood.

"Stay here," said Dolman leaving me alone. While he was gone, I took a moment to enjoy the view of the city. Instead of making me feel powerful, it just made me dizzy.

He returned a few minutes later with a money clip that was straining under the pressure of so many notes.

"Have you found anything?" asked Dolman as he handed over the money.

"Yes, and so far it's not good," I said, wanting to prepare him for the worst. He must have already considered it as he just nodded. I'd expected threats or rage, not this quiet intensity.

"Whatever has happened, find my Selina," he said. "Get me some answers."

"I will," I said, being careful not to make an emotional promise.

I left before he said something else or changed his mind about giving me the money with no strings attached.

Bracken and I retraced our steps across the city to the address that Rose had given us. At first glance, the building looked like many of those around it. A gaudy, brightly painted club or trendy bar. It was only when you walked up to the front door that you noticed something was different. The paint was peeling, the sign was broken and letters were missing. Peering through a gap in the front door, I could just make out the interior. The furniture had been stacked along one side of the room. Chairs, tables and barstools were jumbled together into an impenetrable wall. There was a heavy layer of dust on the floor and an air of abandonment about the place.

A few nights ago, drunk and in a good mood, Selina probably hadn't noticed something was wrong until she was inside. Maybe Rose had shoved her through the front door and walked away. Maybe they'd both gone inside and someone had grabbed her from behind. That way there would be no witnesses. People on the street would have been none the wiser about what had gone on inside.

We circled the building, located the back door and found it was locked with a chain and a heavy padlock. Somehow it mysteriously fell off, and we went inside to check the interior for clues.

After an hour of searching the old club we learned little. The thick dust on the floor had been disturbed by many feet, but it was impossible to track what had happened. Bracken studied the footprints but after a while even he gave up trying to decipher them.

Here's what I think happened. The club had been closed. Rose had been paid to bring Selina to this location, where she'd been abducted by someone. Probably a rival gang, to be used as leverage against her father. If that assumption was true, then where was the ransom note and promise of violence if Dolman didn't comply? And why had someone turned over her apartment? What did she have that was so valuable? Why not just grab her from the Squat Tower? Her father and his goons were too many floors away to hear the noise and come running. Even though Dolman had said she regularly checked in, it was clear they were not as close as he imagined. Maybe it was just lip service on her part, enough to keep him out of her business.

There were a lot of eyeballs on this and a lot of different groups with personal stakes. The warring gangs. The cops. We needed more information.

"Let's try outside," I suggested. The club hadn't yielded anything but perhaps the surrounding streets would give us a few clues.

The early lunchtime crowd was starting to trickle in. Workers seeking a drink or two to help them get through the day. A few desperate prostitutes. Entrepreneurial food sellers with mobile carts. It was a little too early for what I really needed. People were sober and alert. I wanted them loud with loose tongues.

We got some lunch from a decent place I knew not too far away. The owner was reliable, the food was tasty and rich, but not too spicy. Bracken even made a noise of pleasure to show his enjoyment. High praise indeed.

I sent Bracken home for the rest of the afternoon while I went in search of some relief. He would meet me back here at the end of the working day when the bars were heaving with people, desperate for that first post-work drink.

NEW YORK MINUTE

Left to my own devices, I walked away from the bars and clubs, the people and the noise. Although there's no Central Park, there are a few green patches in the paved jungle. It's funny, after only a day or so back in the heart of the city, I found myself craving nature.

I made a beeline for one of the small parks that I'd visited many times in the past. The city was constantly going through facelifts but I was pleased to see that this quiet little corner was exactly the same. A dozen heavy stone tables with wooden inlays on the top were dotted around the space. Grassy verges surrounded the area, where people came to eat their lunch and relax in the sun. At the centre was a small pond and a few small birds pottered about the water. The kiffers were sort of like ducks, but they had blue feet and little red beaks. They beeped and waddled about the tables in search of crumbs, which more than a few of the people were happy to throw their way.

Seven of the twelve tables were occupied by pairs of people so I sat at an empty one. Staring at the black and white chequered board on top, I let my mind wander, trying to find a path through the chaos. After ten minutes of trying to pull it together into some semblance of order, I realised it was no good. I didn't have enough information to see what was really going on.

"You looking for a game, youngster?" someone said.

Looking up, I saw a mature woman with grey hair clutching a narrow wooden box under one arm. "If you've brought your own pieces, I would be delighted," I said.

With a flourish she eased open the top of the box to reveal a beautifully crafted set of chess pieces made of onyx and quartz.

"I'm Cole."

"Marie," she said, shaking my hand. We chose our colours and then set up the pieces. "I hope you're not gonna disappoint me, Cole."

"I have played before," I reassured her.

"Good, but I don't want you letting me win because I'm older than you."

"Marie, I wouldn't dream of it."

"Glad to hear it. All right. Let's get to it," she said, gesturing for me to get on with it.

I whiled away the afternoon playing chess against Marie and then other people in the park, and not once did I think about the chief constable, Dolman, or his daughter.

When the sun began to fade and the lamplighters came out with their poles, everyone packed up and headed for home. The time away left me happier, but now I had to wade back into the case. Bracken met me at the prearranged time and after we'd eaten a quick meal we headed back towards the street where Selina had disappeared.

By the time we got back, the people on the streets around the bars and clubs had swelled. They were standing outside in groups and pairs that had merged into one giant mass of bodies, but there was still room to walk. Later, everyone would be cheek to jowl and getting a drink through the crowd without any spillage would be a challenge.

There was a fuzzy edge to some of the loudest, who were almost shouting in order to be heard. Girls were draped over men like ornaments. Shadows were forming and a general feeling of weariness was starting to creep in. These were just the early-birds. Those dedicated more to work than pleasure. There were tides and habits for everything. The really bad stuff happened much later and with it came a more dangerous crowd of people.

We approached people in the crowd as a pair. I did all the talking and Bracken backed me up as my silent and intimidating partner. Not dispelling anyone of their initial assessment that we were cops, I questioned them without ever needing to show a badge. As expected, most people didn't remember much

NEW YORK MINUTE

about that night. Some had been here. Most had already gone home in search of their beds.

We had better luck with the food sellers. They tended to stay until the bitter end. Until the bars closed and the owners came out for a last bite to eat in the very early hours before they finally went to their beds, often with the dawn.

"There was something happening," said one falafel seller, a middle-aged man with heavy stubble and dark eyes. "A group of people. Couple of women, both of them lookers."

"What were they doing?"

"I don't know. Maybe they were buyers. That place been closed for two months. Places on this street don't really go out of business. Or if they do, they don't stay closed long. Someone else comes along, gives it a new name, a new lick of paint, and they're making money hand over fist. Excuse me," he said, ushering me aside so he could serve another group of drinkers who were suddenly famished.

Beyond that, we had little luck. Someone remembered seeing a tall redheaded woman but that was about it. No one could tell us anything we didn't already know. It was frustrating and a waste of time, but also not unexpected. It was another common occurrence with the job.

"Let's take a walk," I said.

Bracken was glad to leave the crowds behind. He didn't like being around so many people for too long. He preferred solitude and silence to the noise and smells of so many people. More and more every day, I was becoming like that.

As I glanced at the buildings, studying signs and the brickwork above the shops and doorways, Bracken realised what I was looking for. He grunted and joined me in my search. His sharp eyes picked out the first one. It was small. A squiggly line meant to represent a tail curled in a circle. Older tags were present but they'd been scraped off, painted over or defaced. After another hour we'd found six more tags.

"Yellowtails," I said, and Bracken nodded. They were one of the more powerful gangs in the city. Not a challenge for Dolman. Not yet, at least, but they had muscle and in addition to all their seedy sources of revenue, a number of legitimate business ventures. From the looks of it, at the moment at least, that included all of the bars and clubs on the street where Selina had last been seen. It wasn't much, but it was also the first real clue that pointed us towards a specific gang.

Unlike Dolman they didn't have a veneer of civility. They were gutter-punks. Like the Warlords, but with twenty years of experience. Brutal, nasty, and with a feral, rat-like intelligence that only a fool would underestimate. I didn't know who the leader was at present, but in my time, it had been a man named Klein.

Even if Klein was still in charge, I couldn't just march up to him and start asking him questions. It was more likely that he would kill me for mentioning his rival's name than listen to anything I had to say.

We headed towards Bracken's place at a steady walk.

"Why now?" I asked Bracken. "Why would someone grab Selina now?"

He shrugged, not having an answer.

Dolman wasn't about to retire. He'd said that one day Tony would take over the business but he didn't seem in any rush to step away. Had her kidnapping been triggered because something else was about to happen? Was he planning to take out a rival or perhaps move into a new area? I could ask the question but I had the feeling Dolman wouldn't tell me the answer. No. The next time I met him face to face, I needed to have something solid. Some proof that she was alive, or at least who was responsible.

"Why take her and not Tony? Selina isn't the heir," I said, thinking aloud.

"Favourite child?" suggested Bracken.

"Dolman doesn't strike me as the sentimental type. Besides, he's got a new wife. New kids."

"Maybe the wife doesn't like his other kids," he said.

I'd considered it. A jealous new wife, seeing her children as secondary. Neither of them would be old enough to run any part of the business for years. It was possible that she was just cleaning house to set them up for the future, but it seemed a stretch.

With a sigh I gestured to a street on our left, taking us away from Bracken's house. He stopped in the middle of the street and raised an eyebrow.

"There's one person who has more information about what happened. We need to know."

We were fumbling along in the dark. Bracken knew who I meant and what might be required to get the information.

"Lead the way," he said, after barely a pause.

That was one of the reasons he was my best friend and someone I could rely on, no matter what.

It was time to visit Rose again. She knew who had hired her. That name would get us one step closer to the truth and this time, we weren't going to take no for an answer.

CHAPTER 10

Luck, or maybe it was something else, meant that when we arrived at Rose's home it was in time to see her entering the building. At first, I didn't recognise her because of the way she was dressed. It was Bracken who pointed her out. Previously she'd shown me two of her faces. The teasing seducer, and the emotionless reptile that lived beneath the make-up. The one that gave no thought about the wellbeing of other people. This was someone else. In loose cotton trousers and a baggy floral shirt, with her hair tied back and clunky open-toed sandals, she resembled a well-to-do housewife from Queens.

She was toting a couple of bags and she trundled up the stairs and went inside. We waited a couple of minutes to let her get settled and to see if she came back out of the building. I had hoped that we could follow her to one of her rendezvous and disrupt her business. It would be impossible to catch her off guard in her own home, but on the streets it was a different story. After ten minutes I realised she was in for the night so we knocked on the front door and waited.

When Rose answered and saw who it was, her smile wavered. She had no chance of reading Bracken to determine the purpose of our visit. His face was like carved stone. So, of course, she turned to me, but I'd spent the last ten minutes burying my emotions. Even so, Rose must have caught a glimmer of something in my eyes as she tried to close the door on us.

Bracken's hand shot out before she could slam it in our

faces. Rather than wrestle us for control and rely on brute force, she stepped back, retreating in a hurry. While I closed the front door Bracken went after her. By the time I arrived, he was already sitting on the couch in her front room and Rose was pacing, her face flushed and angry.

"What do you want?" she asked.

For a moment, I said nothing and just looked at her. There was something different about her and it wasn't just her appearance. I wasn't nearly as proficient at reading people as Rose, but I could sense something, other than us barging into her apartment, had upset her.

"What?" she asked, catching me staring.

"What's happened, Rose?" I said, ignoring her question.

Her walls went up inside and her eyes became opaque, but it was too late. Buried deep, beneath the layers of selfishness, greed, wrath and envy, I'd seen it. Guilt.

Somehow, what we had said to her about Selina had left an impression, and on some level, she now regretted her actions. Rose might have broken many hearts, and relieved women of their fortunes in their quest to get in her pants, but I didn't get the impression that she had killed anyone in cold blood.

"Who hired you?" I asked, sitting down beside Bracken on the sofa.

Rose paced, working off some energy. She was no longer really angry with us. Maybe she was angry with herself for showing us that she was capable of caring and saw it as a weakness. She muttered something to herself and eventually sat opposite us.

Unlike last time she was not in control, of the situation or the narrative. It showed in her posture which was more neutral and less open. I'd seen a part of her that few people had and she didn't like it.

"Talk," said Bracken.

He didn't need to threaten her. I think a part of her wanted to help us. Part that she thought was dead and buried. That was what had really made her angry. That she wasn't as tough and emotionless as she thought. That she was human, just like the rest of us.

"You need to pay me," said Rose, shrugging. "Nothing in this life is free."

It had the sound of a mantra that someone had told her a long time ago. Something she'd said hundreds of times over the intervening years.

I took out a fifty dollar bill and dropped it on the table between us. Rose folded it up and tucked it into her pocket. Sitting back, she seemed to deflate, becoming smaller, and another layer of her façade melted away. The woman sitting opposite was tired and, I think, looking for a change.

"I received a letter from a guy, even though he knew that I'm exclusive with women. He said it was purely a business arrangement and I was intrigued. Sometimes a middleman will approach me on behalf of a rich client when discretion is required." Rose began to twist a strand of her hair around her finger but there was nothing sensual about it. I had the impression this was one of her tics and not a performance.

"Where did you meet?" I asked, hoping for a clue.

"At a coffee shop. It was busy so no one could hear our conversation. He wanted to make sure I felt safe." Rose smiled at that. We all knew she could take care of herself. "He explained the job, seduce Selina, be her friend and make her want me. After that, all I had to do was deliver her to the club."

"Did you know this man? Did he give you a name?" I asked, sitting forward.

"I didn't recognise him. Not at first, but there was something familiar about him. It was niggling at the back of my mind. You both grew up in the city, right?"

I nodded. "Yeah, why?"

Rose slipped off her sandals and tucked her legs under her,

making herself smaller. Feeling a sudden chill, although the day was still warm, she pulled a shrug over her shoulders.

"You ever hear about the Seventh Avenue massacre?"

I exchanged a look with Bracken. "It's a legend."

Twenty years ago, when we were young men with big balls, we'd heard the story doing the rounds. At the time, I thought it was both amazing and terrifying.

One night in late summer, two gangs, the Serpents and the Kodiaks, turned up on Seventh Avenue to fight for territory. A deal had been struck. Each side was only supposed to bring twelve men. They would settle it the old way. The last man standing took all for his gang.

Both groups stuck to the rule, but the Serpents brought crossbows instead of blades. Half of the Kodiak gang died in the first five seconds. What followed was a vicious and brutal fight. Eventually only one Kodiak was left against seven Serpents. He should have run. He should have died. It should have been a forgone conclusion. But with a blade in each hand, he butchered the seven Serpents and won the day for his gang. There were legends about the man known only as Michael Box.

The reason I thought it was an urban legend was that no one could tell me anything about Box. A couple of years after that, the Kodiak gang was merged into a different gang, and a few years later, that was folded into another one. In the early days, the fighting had been more vicious and gangs were always losing bodies. So there was an endless churn as gangs shrunk and changed their names to keep their numbers.

I was certain it was a myth. It had been invented to inspire young men and women who wanted to join a gang. The story had been carefully crafted by someone to stress the importance of loyalty to your gang and bravery in the face of overwhelming odds. It was also there to fire the imagination. To boost egos and inflate heads that were already swollen with arrogance. It also fed into the common idea among the young of being invulnerable and immortal.

"It's a myth," said Bracken, breaking the silence. "It never happened."

"I always thought that as well. For years. Except it did," said Rose. "The guy I met used to be a Kodiak. Then he became an Ironmonger. Then a Redbane and finally, a Dragon."

A shiver ran down my spine and I felt something click into place inside my head.

"The guy I met works for Karl Dolman. He said his name was Box, but I've seen him around. I know him with another name."

"Booker," I said. The other two looked at me, astonished. Bracken even went so far as to raise both eyebrows which, coming from him, was practically a scream. "Booker is Michael Box."

"Yes," said Rose.

I had thought Booker was nothing more than an over the hill fighter. Someone past his prime who Dolman kept around out of a sense of loyalty. It might have been that, but it was also something more. Booker was one of the architects of Dolman's criminal empire. If Booker had been around the streets for that long, he had to be one of Dolman's earliest followers. With his reputation and penchant for violence, Booker had helped his boss carve out territory while filling the gutters with blood. I had known Booker was a killer. That much had been obvious the first time we'd met, but I'd had no idea who he really was.

"What will you do?" asked Rose, hugging herself.

"I have no idea," I admitted.

"We squeeze him for information," said Bracken, as if it would be that easy. With him at my side, maybe it would be.

We left Rose and took to the streets while I tried to make sense of it all. Even if Booker wasn't the infamous Michael Box, I was struggling to understand why he had turned on his boss. He obviously had affection for Selina, the portrait in his office was evidence of that, and had probably been around since her birth, so he'd seen her grow up from a girl into a woman. All of that combined with decades of loyalty to her father meant he was practically family to Karl Dolman.

"Why would he betray Dolman?" I asked, thinking aloud.

Bracken didn't answer, leaving me to work it through in my head. He led and I followed, my mind elsewhere, as we traversed the streets. There were only a few reasons I could think of that would make Booker betray those closest to him.

"Bad debt," suggested Bracken, ticking off his fingers. "A threat to family. A dark secret."

"Darker than the Seventh Avenue massacre?" I asked. "I don't think it's money. If he'd gambled himself into a deep hole, I think Dolman would bail him out for the sake of old times."

Money didn't feel right. It had to be far more personal.

"Kidnapping," said Bracken.

I had no idea if Booker was married and had children, but it was possible. Given his age, maybe someone had kidnapped a beloved granddaughter and was holding her ransom. Maybe it was the Yellowtails, as Selina had been delivered to the abandoned club in their territory.

"There's only one way to find out," I said with a sigh. Bracken adjusted the gloves on his hands.

It was late and we had been standing around for a couple of hours waiting for Booker to emerge from the Squat Tower. Stakeouts are dull affairs where your own boredom works against you.

At the start, I was watching the door for movement. Every time someone emerged from the building, my heart leapt into action, adrenaline filled my bloodstream and I prepared myself for a brutal fight. But it was never Booker and by the twentieth time someone stepped out, I had stopped reacting. The fight or flight instinct had become numb to surprise. I also stopped staring at the door and started to glance around the street, giving a person plenty of time to leave the building without me noticing. That's why you always have to work in a pair on a job like this.

After half an hour, when I started to drift off, Bracken took over and I leaned against the wall in the shadows, resting my eyes and letting my heartbeat return to normal. When he got tired we switched again.

About when I was ready to give it up as a lost cause, Booker came out of the front door. At first, I didn't react. I knew it was him. I recognised him, but my brain and instincts were numb and slow. I nudged Bracken, who stepped forward and I pointed. He nodded and set off in pursuit, staying at a distance while trying to keep our prey in sight. Despite the hour, and only patches of people on the streets, it was a challenge. Too close and he'd know we were there. Too far behind and we could lose him when he turned a street corner.

Once the Squat Tower, and the imminent threat of reprisal from Dolman was behind us, we stepped up the pace. If Booker knew we were there, he gave no sign and continued to amble along without any concern. When he turned the next corner and disappeared from view, Bracken put a hand on my chest, stopping me in my tracks.

"He knows," he said.

"No point in hiding, then," I said and we sped up to a fast walk.

Booker was waiting for us halfway down the road. Standing with his back to us as he scanned the nearby buildings. The windows were all dark. There would be no witnesses for whatever transpired.

It was only when we drew near that he bothered to turn and face us.

"You," he said with surprise. Booker glanced at Bracken,

but showed no signs of recognition. Even so, he frowned. The odds of two against one meant nothing to him. It was the fact that Bracken was a complete unknown that bothered him. "What do you want?"

"Why did you do it?" I asked. "Why did you betray Dolman?"

Booker shook his head. "You don't know what you're talking about."

"I know who you are," I said.

He shrugged. "Even so, if you knew all the things I've done, you'd never ask that question."

"You betrayed Selina. Who hired you to abduct her?"

Booker's expression finally changed, but he wasn't angry, more disappointed. "Walk away. If you stay, it will cost your life."

I knew it wasn't an idle threat. Even in his current condition, which was far past his prime, there was something primal and dangerous lurking just beneath his skin. And once it rose up he wouldn't be able to hold it in check. On my own, I wouldn't have lasted a minute. Thankfully, I was a lot smarter than him.

"Blade or fists," said Bracken, taking off his jacket.

Booker grinned. "Old school. I like it. Fists, of course," he said.

I started to take off my jacket as well but Bracken shook his head. "You cannot."

He knew I couldn't win against such a bruiser by myself, but with two of us the odds were better. "Why?"

"I don't want to hurt you," he said.

The Slate was changing him. It wasn't just making him immune to pain. It was altering his body in ways no one understood. Bracken had been holding back when he'd fought against the Warlords and his punches had still bordered on lethal. Against such a seasoned fighter as Booker, he would have to let go. Anything less would be a mistake and might result in his death.

Bracken adjusted his gloves to make sure they were on tight and then stepped forward to meet Booker. The bruiser's fist slammed into his side but my old friend didn't react. Two crosses from Bracken split his lip. A series of jabs bloodied his nose and split the skin over one eye, but Booker just soaked it up and grinned through bloody teeth.

"Don't hold back," said Booker. I could see he was desperate to release what had been caged for so long. I thought he might come to regret those words as Bracken clubbed him on the right side of his head. I heard something crack and the big man spun sideways, collided with the wall but, somehow, stayed on his feet. Booker came out fighting, swinging while covering his head which left his body exposed. Bracken took a few punches to the face, a couple of shots to the ribs, and when he barely reacted to the body blows, I saw Booker's frown deepen.

The hesitation cost him. Two jabs from Bracken snapped his head back so hard I thought it had broken his neck, but Booker just took a few steps and fell onto his arse.

"Talk," said Bracken, spitting blood.

The old bruiser just shook his head and pushed himself upright.

Then he let go of everything.

From a young age, we are taught to toe the line and observe social niceties. Every facet of our lives depends on our willingness to submit to the rules. Every day, we bury the savage parts of our nature. The primal version of ourselves. Our dark, ancestral heart.

Walk, don't run. Be polite. Don't cheat. Don't steal. Don't talk back. Respect your parents. Don't raise your voice. Don't get angry. Don't fight. Don't kill.

But what are we when all of that is gone?

NEW YORK MINUTE

Stripped of everything that had been holding him back, Booker went after my best friend without restraint.

Bracken was sent reeling by a savage flurry of blows and was not given any time to recover. I could not stand by and watch him get beaten to death, but when I stepped forward Booker was right there in front of me. His fist caught me on the jaw, and before the pain had registered, my world went black. I came awake a few seconds later, looking up at them.

Booker fought to kill and made no attempt to protect himself from potential injuries. There was a wild glee in his eyes that told me how much he was relishing the spray of blood, the crunch of bone, the hammer of fist on flesh. He panted and snarled like a wild beast.

Bracken was silent. His mouth pulled into a firm line which I thought meant that he was focused and calm. Instead, I caught a glimpse of his face and it made me terribly afraid for him. There was a dullness behind his eyes. A lack of clarity that told me he was fighting through instinct, not thought. I feared the Slate had entered his mind and stolen his wits.

As Booker's fists came towards him at speed, Bracken responded in kind, unleashing his strength without restraint.

It was brutal and vicious and horrific to watch. Both of them hit each other so hard that every strike spelled out a potentially life-threatening injury. The only reason Bracken could stand up to such punishment was the Slate.

And then it was over.

A left cross from Bracken knocked out three of Booker's teeth. A right gut shot made him spit blood. A follow through bent him double and a left jab shattered the ocular bones around the bruiser's eye socket. He fell to the street and this time, Booker didn't get back up.

He was spattered with blood. One eye swollen shut. The other misshapen from the broken bones. His lips were fat and torn, and he wheezed like someone who had run a marathon.

Bracken stumbled towards him and I put myself between them.

"It's over," I said into that gulf of silence. "It's done," I stress, holding Bracken's gaze with my own.

What followed was the longest and worst five seconds of my life. When Bracken stared at me, there was no hint of recognition. It seemed impossible, that after all that we'd been through over the years, my oldest friend didn't know me.

Everyone forgets the little things, and short term memory can be impaired by something as basic as lack of sleep. But old memories, they shine in the dark. Right before she died, my old aunt couldn't remember her name, but she knew exactly what kind of cake she'd baked for my tenth birthday.

Bracken and I were closer than brothers because we'd chosen each other. We'd been there for each other, during the most important moments in our lives. His blank stare terrified me.

Slowly, so slowly, the familiar light came back into his eyes and he knew me again. With a grunt, he stepped back, wiped his face, and spat blood.

I knelt beside Booker, who had rolled onto his side. He was still struggling to get a full breath and had developed a peculiar whistle in his throat. I suspected several ribs were broken and thought one or more might have pierced a lung.

"Who hired you?" I asked, bending forward to hear him speak.

Through bloody lips he muttered a name, and I stumbled back in surprise.

CHAPTER 11

Tired, bloody, and bruised, we ran through the dark streets of New York to try and prevent a massacre.
　With that utterance, Booker had changed everything about the case. Every assumption I had made was wrong. Every clue I had thought was leading me towards a reasonable conclusion was a lie. If we survived, there would be time for analysis. To study where my thinking had been led astray, but only if we lived to see the dawn.
　Bracken was in bad shape. His face was a swollen mass, with cuts, scrapes and one of his eyes half closed. I couldn't be sure but I thought several bones in his face were fractured, if not broken. He was breathing hard and slightly hunched over, suggesting bruised or broken ribs. Gloves concealed the damage to his hands, but I suspect they were also swollen and hurting him. Bracken had endured a beating worse than anything I'd ever seen, and yet when I asked, he ran without complaint. He understood what was at stake if we failed.
　From the beginning I had been willing to entertain the thought that, despite everything I knew about Selina Dolman and her background, she was the victim. That she was just a pawn in someone else's game. Just one piece of a much larger plan. In this, I had been both right and wrong.
　Selina had arranged the whole thing herself.
　The seduction by Rose. Her abduction and, to a degree, my investigation into her disappearance. She had known exactly what her father would do. She had been playing all of us since

the very beginning.

An entrepreneur. That was what Karl Dolman had said about his eldest daughter. That she was different and always wanted to do things her own way. Well, now she was.

As she wasn't Dolman's first-born, Selina would never inherit her father's empire. Part of me suspected that if something had happened to Tony, her father would have passed control to one of his other children instead of her. Dolman had admitted that Selina used to terrify him which, looking back on what he'd said, should have worried me. Hindsight was a stone-cold bitch.

Selina was going to tear it all down and take over. Become the queen of her own empire, built on the blood of her family. If her older brother, Tony, wasn't already dead, I suspected he would be soon. My guess was that she'd made a deal with the leader of the Yellowtails, or had just taken over, and they would be the muscle that helped bring about her father's downfall. Once her father and Tony were dead, she would have to kill her half-brother and sister. She didn't want them coming after her in ten years as adults, seeking revenge for the death of their parents.

We ran. To save Karl Dolman, of all people, from being murdered, but also his children. It wasn't their fault their father was a maniac. They still had the potential to be something else. There would be other innocents, of course, caught in the middle, their innards splattered up the walls. People guilty of nothing more than being in the wrong place at the wrong time.

Selina knew everything about her father's business. Even worse, she had Booker on the inside, feeding her information, maybe leaving a few doors unlocked on his way out of the building. It would be a massacre.

By the time we arrived at the entrance to the Squat tower, I knew were already too late. The bloodshed had begun. Two Yellowtails were hunkered down just inside the shadowy entrance, their bright yellow mohawks almost glowing in the dark. They came to their feet as we ran towards them. Each held a bloody knife.

I drew my Colt short sword and, for the first time, Bracken took out the big knife from behind his back. We fought in silence while they spat and swore. They were wily, skinny and vicious, used to fighting other criminals, many of whom lacked skill. As a cop I'd drilled for hundreds of hours until fighting became instinctive. Long before that, Bracken and I had run through the streets carrying knives, playing gangster. We'd fought other kids in the neighbourhood with fists, sticks, rocks and later knives. We'd been kings of the castle until we met someone bigger, stronger and tougher than us who gave us a thrashing. We'd learned some hard lessons along the way and had the scars to prove it.

As the Yellowtail jabbed at me, I stepped to the side and brought my sword down on his forearm. The blade severed his hand and he stared in shock at the bloody stump before the colour drained from his face. With a lunge I punched the tip of the blade into his throat and back out, ending his life. He could have survived losing a hand, but it was better not to leave an enemy at my back.

Bracken had his blade buried in the Yellowtail's chest. With a sharp wrench he pulled it out. The fight had taken less than a minute and we had no time to waste. There was still a long climb ahead to the top of the building.

Moving quickly, we jogged up the stairs before settling into a steady rhythm as it was a long way to the top floor. The lights in the walls flickered, like a fading heartbeat. As if the huge beast we'd entered was dying. I knew it was nothing more than my imagination. That it was the technology breaking down, but the thought wouldn't leave me. My thighs began to burn, my heart was pounding, and sweat trickled down my back. Bracken was huffing beside me but we both pressed on. I was desperate to stop and rest but even a short break could cost lives.

With every step, I cursed Dolman for living on the top floor. Only someone like him, with a big ego and so much money, would want to be so high up. So that he could stare down at us, as if he were a ruler surveying his kingdom.

On the twelfth floor, two before we reached the top, I gestured at the door and Bracken followed me through. Booker's office was on this floor and I thought it might be wise to try and sneak in rather than go through the front door. The rest of the floor was used for office and storage space. In some rooms, I saw crates stacked floor to ceiling. Another contained bags of dried goods, sacks of rice and other pulses. There were random pieces of furniture covered in cloths, a dining table, chairs and several offices, all of which were empty. Two of them showed signs of a disturbance, with paper scattered across the floor, upturned furniture and an unpleasant smell coming from one of them. I saw someone's foot sticking out from under the desk but we didn't stop to investigate. There was nothing to be done to help them.

The door to Booker's office was closed but a short distance away, we saw signs of a fight. There had been a bloody and violent battle leading up to the back stairs. There were deep gouges on the walls and blood had been splashed liberally across the floor. I could see boot prints, all of them going in the same direction: towards the narrow stairs.

The Yellowtails had snuck in this way.

At the bottom of the stairs we found Caleb. He was on the floor with his back resting against the door. His hands were in his lap and his head bent forward, chin resting on his chest. I wished that he was just resting, catching a quick nap, but he was sitting in a pool of blood. It had already soaked into the material of his trousers and there was more on the walls. His arms were covered with cuts and scratches. His shirt was stained red and he was missing two fingers on his left hand.

He'd been surprised and fought hard, doing his best to stem the tide, but inevitably, he'd been overwhelmed. A closer look showed five puncture wounds in his chest. He had not gone down easily.

"No time," said Bracken, touching my shoulder. "Mourn later."

I nodded and pressed on. We drew our weapons as we went up the back stairs, ears strained for the slightest noise. On the fourteenth floor, the door had been ripped off its hinges. It lay in the middle of the plush hallway and scattered around it were half a dozen bodies, both Yellowtails and Dolman's guards. The blood had barely congealed, which meant this had happened recently.

It wasn't long before I heard the clang of steel and the screams of dying men and women, fighting for their lives.

Slowing to a walk, we crept forward, muscles taut. Now was not the time to race around a corner and land in the middle of a fight without any warning.

Every door on the corridor had been shoved open or kicked in. Each room had been trashed, with cupboard doors ripped open and wardrobes emptied of all clothing. At first, I couldn't work out what they were looking for, and then it came to me. The Yellowtails were making sure there were no spaces where a child might hide. My worst fear was coming true. Selina intended to murder her half brother and sister.

We paused at a T-junction, trying to decide which way to turn as there were sounds of battle coming from both directions.

"There," said Bracken, tilting his head to the right. I heard a woman scream, not in anger, but from fear and dread. An innocent bystander. One of Dolman's staff or perhaps his wife.

A short distance away, we came across a Yellowtail standing in a doorway with their back to us. There was some commotion inside the room. The heavy thump of bodies moving and coarse, mocking laughter suggested something unpleasant. Bracken clamped one hand over the Yellowtail's mouth and drove his blade into their back with the other. The woman dropped to the floor without a sound and we stepped into the room.

Two Yellowtails were cutting off Mrs Dolman's hair.

The room was decorated like a barber shop, with lots of mirrors on the walls and a huge swivel chair in the centre of the room. There was a sink on the left and a set of shelves on the right in disarray. Once it might have contained the barber's tools of the trade, scissors, combs and coloured glass bottles of hair tonic. Now the implements were scattered across the floor, and the sink was full of broken glass.

The room smelled of hair gel and chemicals. Mrs Dolman was in the chair, being held from behind by one of the Yellowtails. He had a hand around her throat and was choking her, while the other cut off her hair with a pair of scissors. The floor was covered with her blonde hair. Her face was twisted into a vicious snarl and she wore only a silk nightdress.

Our appearance distracted the Yellowtails so she bit the one who was holding her, sinking her teeth into the meat of the man's hand.

With a shriek of pain he released his grip and tried to shake her loose. A bite became the least of his concerns as Bracken slashed him across the face with his knife. I went after the other, who stumbled back, tripped over his own feet and fell against the wall. I followed with sword, driving it through his chest, pinning him in place.

"Stay here," I said to Mrs Dolman. I wasn't sure if she recognised me but she shook her head.

"My children are out there," she said, picking up one of the dead men's blades. From the way she held it I knew it wasn't her first time wielding a sword. "Go!"

Bracken shrugged. Short of knocking her unconscious, there

was no way to stop her from following us. Even if we took the time to hide her in a cupboard, she was still at risk. Selina and her people could not leave her alive. A widow was a powerful symbol and a great motivator for any who survived.

"Just stay back," I said, not knowing if she would listen.

At the end of the hallway, we encountered a melee. Eight Yellowtails were battling against four of Dolman's men. I recognised some of them from my previous visits, and all of them were carrying big Roman-style shields. When they locked them together, they filled most of the hallway, creating an impenetrable wall, which was the only reason they were still alive. The Yellowtails were trying to shove them back, while poking at them with spears. Two crossbow bolts were stuck in one shield but no one had a bow, which made things easier.

Pulling on my punching dagger, I nodded to Bracken and we ran into the fight, coming up behind the Yellowtails. I'd crippled two of them before they noticed we were there, punching one in the kidney and another in the spine. While they bled and squealed, I hacked at the others with my sword. Bracken punched one man so hard in the side of the face it shattered his jaw, spraying teeth and pieces of bone everywhere. His knife went into the throat of another. A warm spray of blood crossed my face.

"Fucking die!" shrieked Mrs Dolman, using her sword with both hands like an axe. She chopped at one man's shoulder so hard she shattered his collar bone. Dolman's men took advantage of the distraction, lowered their shields and came forward. We crushed the Yellowtails between us and made short work of those who were still standing.

"Where are my children?" said Mrs Dolman. "Where is my husband?"

"We don't know," said one of the men. He had a stained bandage wrapped around his head and another on his arm. Mrs Dolman started arguing with the men so I took a minute to catch my breath.

"Cole." The tone of Bracken's voice cut through the noise and I looked up to see where he was pointing. At the far end of the corridor were at least a dozen Yellowtails. All bigger and meaner than the others we had faced. All scarred veterans. The conversation behind me dried up and the two groups stared at one another in silence. They seemed to be waiting for something and a little while later, I saw the reason.

The ranks of the Yellowtails parted and Selina Dolman walked to the front of the group. Despite the top of her head barely reaching the shoulder of the tallest Yellowtail, it was obvious she was in charge. The thugs moved aside out of fear and respect. I could see the concern on their faces, as if a dangerous beast from the Wild was standing in their midst.

Selina had long jet-black hair and dark brooding eyes like her father. Thankfully, she must have inherited her looks from her mother. Were it not for the fact that she was a violent psychopath, I would have said she was an attractive woman. She was dressed in tight black trousers and a matching black vest that showed off her athletic figure and toned arms. She moved with a feline grace that told me her bulk was lean muscle not fat.

There was a worrying gleam in Selina's eyes. It was the same one I'd seen in her father's.

"You ungrateful bitch," spat Mrs Dolman, which made Selina smile.

"Fifty grand to whoever brings me her head," she said, before turning and walking away.

"We're outnumbered," I said to one of Dolman's men. "If we're going to stand a chance against them, we need a more defensive position. Is there somewhere nearby?"

He considered it a second and then nodded. "Yeah, maybe."

I hoped an answer would come to him, but honestly, anywhere was better than our current position.

"Get ready to move," I whispered to the others, before grabbing Mrs Dolman by the wrist. She gave me a look nasty enough to curdle milk, but I didn't let go. "If you want to see your children, you'll do as I say."

She glanced at my hand on her arm and this time, I let go. "I remember you," she muttered. "My husband will cut off your balls and feed them to you for touching me."

I could have said something vicious about the unlikelihood that her husband was still alive, or that any of us were going to get out of here. Instead, I bit my tongue and tried to remember that she was relatively innocent and the sort of person I was supposed to be saving.

"What about the kitchen?" said one Dolman's men. He and the one with the bandage were still discussing defensive positions.

"For fuck's sake," said Mrs Dolman. "Troy, lead us to the dining room."

"Oh yeah, good idea," said Troy, adjusting the bandage on his head.

Just as the Yellowtails came forward, we withdrew, running at full speed, jumping over obstacles, dodging bodies, skidding through pools of blood that had soaked into the carpet.

At first, I thought Mrs Dolman had led us into a dead end as we arrived at the room where I'd eaten with the family. While Dolman's men flipped over the dining table and stacked the chairs to create a barrier, Mrs Dolman went towards the bookshelves.

"Help me with this," she said, gesturing at me and Bracken. Reaching behind one of the books, she twisted something and the bookshelf shifted on a set of concealed hinges. Doing my best to ignore the damage to the books, we pulled the bookcase to one side, revealing a narrow corridor barely wide enough for one person.

"Where does this go?" I asked.

"There is a spiral staircase at the end of the corridor. It goes down two floors and come out near Booker's office," she explained.

"Did he know about it?"

Mrs Dolman gave me a weird look. "No. Why?" she said, and I heaved a sigh of relief. If he had been aware, we could have been walking into another trap.

There was no time to talk as the Yellowtails burst into the room, screaming bloody murder. I joined the others at the barricade and yelled back in defiance, lashing out with jabs that didn't cause severe damage but inflicted pain. Our attackers recoiled, spat and swore as we kept them at a distance. A large, scarred Yellowtail ran at us in a frenzy. Using her body as a shield, two others followed in her wake.

Without restraint, Bracken's fist smashed into her face so hard it snapped her head back and she was dead by the time she hit the floor.

It was brutal and horrific work, slicing and gouging, hurling insults to hold back the fear as we all battled to stay alive. The man next to me went down and I took the shield from his blood-slicked fingers before he was dead. Using the steel boss at the centre of the shield, I rammed it into the face of one woman and stabbed another Yellowtail through the eye with my punching dagger. He recoiled in horror, screeched in agony and dropped to his knees.

"Just die!" someone shouted next to me and I heard a wheeze that faded from someone else as if they accommodated the request.

A Yellowtail in front of me went down, and then another. Something clipped me on the side of the head and I toppled backwards to the floor. I expected to be stabbed as the barrier was overcome, but the thugs around me slumped against the table with relief.

The fight was over.

NEW YORK MINUTE

The air was thick with the stench of ripe fear sweat, blood, shit and bodies. My heart was pounding, my skin slick with sweat and lungs burning. Everyone was gasping, but this far up none of the windows opened and the stench was trapped. A few of the Yellowtails were still alive but injured, and three of Dolman's men were on the ground. Two were dead and the third looked as if he would soon join them. I hadn't realised it, but Mrs Dolman had been in the thick of the fight. Her elegant nightwear, much like her skin, was splattered with blood and filth. The fourth man was moving among the bodies of the Yellowtails, ruthlessly finishing all of them off by stabbing them through the heart. Despite the weight, I kept hold of the shield. In such melees there was little room for swinging a sword and some protection was better than none.

"We need to find your husband and children. Where did you last see him?" I asked.

"He was in his study," said Mrs Dolman, wiping the blood from her face, "but we passed it on the way here."

"Then where would he go?"

A growing sense of horror crept over Mrs Dolman's face. Without saying a word she ran from the room and we followed, leaving the dead behind.

If there were other battles elsewhere in the building, we couldn't hear them and an eerie silence filled the corridors that made me nervous. The sound of our footfalls was absorbed by the plush carpets which was a relief. If we ran into any more Yellowtails, or Selina Dolman, they wouldn't hear us coming.

At the far end of the corridor was the children's playroom. It was a huge space, at least as big as my entire apartment, and it was filled with stacks of toys, stuffed animals and games. One wall was covered with shelves which held more personal items that the children had made. Roughly made figurines carved from wood and moulded from clay. A crude painting of the city, and propped up against the wall was the most ruthless man in New York, Karl Dolman.

The big man was dead. Both of his hands had been hacked off with an axe. Someone had gone to the effort of nailing them to the far wall. They would have been in view until he lost consciousness, adding insult to brutal injury. It felt personal, as if whoever was responsible had been sending a message, and I knew that Selina had done the deed herself. Dolman was no saint, far from it, but to be killed in this way, in his own home, by his daughter, was a nasty way to go. He probably deserved it, for the misery his drugs and gangs had inflicted on the city, but I didn't get any satisfaction from seeing it.

Mrs Dolman crouched beside her husband in her blood-soaked nightdress and placed a hand on his shoulder.

"Guuh," said Dolman, scaring the shit out of everyone.

Somehow, he was still alive. His head came up and he stared around the room with bloodshot eyes that wouldn't focus.

"Karl, I'm here," said Mrs Dolman, stroking her husband's cheek. The tone of her voice eased the lines of pain etched into his face, but only for a moment.

"Selina," he rasped.

"Save your strength," she said, as if he had a chance of surviving. I glanced at Bracken and he shook his head. There was no way to come back from losing both hands. Dolman had already lost too much blood, and if not that, then the shock would kill him. "Where are the children?" she asked.

In spite of everything, Dolman grinned, showing his teeth. He whispered something and his wife sagged with relief.

"Find them!" someone shouted, their voice echoing down the empty hallways. It was Selina. Frantic, thirsting for the blood of her siblings. She would never be able to relax unless they were dead at her feet.

Bracken and Troy were keeping watch at the door. There was no sign of anyone yet, but I knew we didn't have much time.

"Help me get him on his feet," said Mrs Dolman, expecting me to follow her orders.

"If we move him, he'll die," I said, not pointing out that he was already a dead man. She knew the truth, she just didn't want to accept it. Living this life, marrying Karl Dolman, she had no illusions about the kind of man he was and what his business entailed. The risk of death was never far away, although she probably hadn't thought it would happen like this. Slowly bleeding to death in their own home, surrounded by their kids' toys and board games. Perhaps she'd imagined him going out in a blaze of glory. Facing countless enemies by himself. Etching his name onto the bloody ledger of history until he became a bogeyman that parents used to get their children to obey. Do as you're told or Karl Dolman will come for you!

For all his power, all his money and influence, there was one enemy that even Dolman couldn't hope to control or defeat: death. She broke all the rules. There was no way to bribe her and no deal could ever be struck. She was the great leveller. Heroes died young on the toilet. Cowards lived to see old age. And gangsters bled to death for the countless sins of their past.

"Cole, we're out of time," said Bracken. So many words from him was unusual and the strain of the situation even showed on his face. He knew we were seconds away from being overwhelmed. Dolman heaved a final breath and his chin dropped forward onto his chest for the last time.

"We have to move," I said, not wanting to rush Mrs Dolman but knowing that every second we stayed could mean our deaths. Although reluctant to leave him, Mrs Dolman let me pull her upright. "We need to find your children."

That made her focus on the present. She would mourn later. Her jaw tightened and her eyes narrowed. "Follow me."

Leaving Dolman behind to face whatever came next, we went in search of his young children.

CHAPTER 12

Selina and her gang of Yellowtails were tearing the floor apart in their desperate search to find her siblings.

Every room we passed had been thoroughly destroyed. Every cupboard door torn off and the contents strewn about. Every piece of furniture shredded to make sure they weren't hiding inside or underneath. Floorboards had been ripped up. Walls punctured, in case they contained hiding spaces. A lot of the damage seemed to be driven by rage as much as desperation. The longer this went on, the more attention it would attract.

Eventually the authorities might get involved, but then again, probably not, as it was fairly self-contained and the number of civilian casualties would be minimal. But there were other gangs in the city and such a major shift of power would attract them like files to a freshly squeezed turd. The best I could hope for was that the police would keep others out of the Squat Tower to prevent it from becoming a charnel house. There were some residents on the lower floors who had no idea what went on in the penthouse, but they would soon find out. When this was over it would be difficult for anyone not to notice the dead bodies being carried down the stairs.

In every room that we passed, the number of lives lost became increasingly apparent. Three of Dolman's bodyguards here. Six there. Four Yellowtails stuffed into a bath. Five beheaded and dumped in a jumbled pile of limbs. Once I reached one hundred, I stopped counting. The death toll on

NEW YORK MINUTE

both gangs was staggering and still it wasn't over.

As Mrs Dolman led us along the floor I could hear fighting elsewhere, and on two separate occasions we met groups of Yellowtails. We silenced them before they could call for reinforcements but the clock was also ticking. Eventually Selina and her people would find the children and then they would shift their attention towards us.

We came across a knot of three Yellowtails fighting four of Dolman's people and brought the fight to a sudden conclusion. With five bodyguards surrounding Mrs Dolman, I felt better about our odds. All of them were wounded but still able to fight. These were the most experienced, the most skilled and the toughest of his people. They followed her orders without question and to my surprise, she led us towards a door we had passed earlier.

It was a storage room and had contained various cleaning products on shelves, paint, mops and brooms. Now it was a tangled mess of wood. The floor splattered with dented paint tins and splinters of wood. All of the shelves had been torn down and the walls gouged but they were solid wood. Before I could ask the question, we heard people approaching and readied ourselves for another fight. Thankfully, it was another four of Dolman's people bringing their total up to nine, which made an even dozen with Mrs Dolman and us.

While they tended their wounds and tightened makeshift bandages, I leaned against the wall to catch my breath. After his fight with Booker and then this, Bracken must have been exhausted but he said nothing, just squatted and took a moment to rest. I was certain that most of the blood on his clothes and face wasn't his own. Even so, I was worried about the cumulative effect on him after such a brutal day. We weren't young men anymore who could fight all day, drink all night and be fresh the next morning.

As if he knew that I was worrying, Bracken looked up and

offered a brief smile.

Mrs Dolman stepped into the cupboard and then turned around, facing out. Reaching above her head she pressed part of the wall and I heard a faint click.

"Help me with this," she said, clearing a space on the floor so we could both step into the narrow cupboard. There was just enough room for us to stand shoulder to shoulder. With our hands braced against the back wall we pushed and the whole wall moved backwards on oiled runners. Because of the weight, it was not easy to move and the tired muscles in my legs began to complain. The rails swerved to the right and the section of the wall slid out of the way to reveal a set of metal stairs. I smelled fresh air before I saw the hatch at the top of the short staircase.

Carrying a lamp, Mrs Dolman ran up the stairs and disappeared through the hatch. Moving cautiously I followed up the stairs and then outside.

To my surprise I found that we were on the roof of the Squat Tower. I suspected few people had been up here before and I found it both terrifying and exhilarating. Part of the roof was covered with four banked rows of large glass plates that were deep blue and reflected the light. Several huge machines were connected to the panels with cables as fat as my leg and there was an array of chimneys and metal spikes whose purpose eluded me. There was just enough light from the stars so I didn't trip over any obstacles. The rest was hidden in deep shadow.

"Kids!" shrieked Mrs Dolman. Her voice cracked and some of her words were lost as they were carried away on the wind. I was grateful there was only a slight breeze. Being up here on a stormy day would be a nightmare. There was only a shallow lip around the edge of the roof and I resisted the urge to peer down to the street below.

The view of the city was majestic but I also had an

uncomfortable pain in the pit of my stomach. Part of me was imagining falling to my death from such a great height.

With a cry of relief Mrs Dolman sank to her knees as her two children appeared from their hiding place behind one of the chimneys. Despite the bloody nightdress and partly shaven head, they swarmed over her, crying and babbling at the same time.

I left her and stared down at the streets below. I could see hundreds of lights scattered across the city. Beyond that was a swathe of black nothingness. It was featureless, like a void without stars.

We weren't alone out here. I knew there were other towns and cities but, at that moment, I felt as if New York was alone in the world. Our problems were our own. No one was coming to help us. Rise or fall, the future of the city was ours.

Selina's war with her father would cause a ripple, spreading out from the Squat Tower in all directions. It would bypass some, turn others, and set some down new paths. Countless lives would be changed. Some for the better, many for the worse. Looking at the tear-stained faces of Dolman's kids, I didn't envy their future. The traumas I'd endured in my childhood had left their mark, and I was still dealing with them today. I wondered what they would become without the reassuring presence of their powerful and deadly father.

"Cole," said Bracken, sticking his head out of the hatch. "Selina is here."

Mrs Dolman's head snapped up and her hands tightened into fists.

"Stay here," I said, heading towards the stairs.

At first I thought she was going to ignore me. I knew she could fight. That wasn't in doubt, but right now her children needed her. Besides, I wondered if one more body would really make a difference.

"If she gets past us…" I said, leaving the rest unspoken, and

Mrs Dolman nodded. Selina wouldn't touch them. She'd kill them herself before she let that happen. Maybe jump off the roof with them and take flight. It might be exhilarating to fall so fast, at least until the very last second.

Downstairs, the others were ready, weapons and shields in hand, faces determined. They weren't just fighting to protect the kids. They were fighting to save their own lives. To make matters worse, they were fighting against a traitor. Many of the men and women around me were Dolman's veterans. They'd probably helped build his empire, which meant they'd watched Selina grow up from a sweet girl into a jealous woman. And now here she was, with a gang of Yellowtails at her back, wanting to tear it all down and take over. It was their blood that had paved the way, not hers. She'd been safe and warm, protected by them, night after night, year after year, and this was how she repaid their sacrifice.

They said nothing. No curses or questions about how she could do such a thing. We all knew the reasons: jealousy and greed. It was that simple.

At the far end of the hallway Selina was waiting with her group of Yellowtails. I guessed there was a dozen and I hoped that they were the last of her followers in the tower. If she had more waiting in reserve then we were all dead. As it was, I thought the odds that both Bracken and I would walk away from this fight were slim.

I was relying on those beside me but I didn't care about their survival. I just needed them to make up the numbers. They'd signed on for this sort of thing. Bracken and I were now innocent bystanders, caught between two warring gangs, fighting for our lives.

"Bring out the kids and you can just walk away," said Selina. We all knew it was a lie. She wouldn't let anyone go free and risk being seen as merciful. Her own gang would turn on her if she showed such weakness. That was the world they lived in.

Where compassion and mercy were grave sins not virtues. When no one moved she spat on the carpet, cursing their loyalty to a dead man.

With nothing left to be said, they charged. Hefting the shield in my left hand, sword in my right, I braced myself.

What happened next was not a noble battle. Not a joyous fight for glory and honour. It was savage, visceral and an agonising struggle for survival.

I slammed my shield into one woman's face, shattering her nose. With my right hand I stabbed and hacked, screaming at the Yellowtails. All around me was noise and motion, men and women shouting, grunting, crying out in pain. The air rang with the clash of steel and the stink of fear sweat and blood flooded my nose. People screamed and wailed. Someone called out for their mother.

A body collided with my shield hard enough that it nearly ripped it from my arm. I was knocked off balance, bounced into the man next to me and rebounded back into the fight. I was just in time to stab a man in the face as he raised his sword to cut down one of Dolman's men. The point of my blade entered his body through the armpit, angled up into his chest, and quickly back out. He dropped to the ground and was gone from the fight.

Beside me, Bracken fought in silence. His contempt for the enemy was a palpable force that worried me. His eyes were glazed and he didn't just fight to survive. I'm not sure he was conscious of where he was, only that someone in front of him was standing in his way. He would never surrender. Never back down. The only way to make him stop was to kill him and that was proving to be incredibly difficult. Every blow from his big knife was vicious, maiming and killing. It went through one man's eye. Into the chest of a woman. Sliced another from hip to hip, spilling her innards across the floor.

And then it was over. There was no one standing upright in

front of me anymore. The once plush carpet was now covered with dead and dying bodies, warm innards and gallons of blood. Selina was on one knee, a hand pressed to her side as blood pumped from a wound. There was more blood on her face and a nasty gash down one cheek.

Bracken was rigid, the knife still clenched in one hand. Scattered around me were injured men and women. There were two veterans on our side still upright and the rest were on their backs. Some were dying. A few might live if they saw a doctor, but the rest were already breathing their last.

"It's over," I said, but Bracken didn't respond. I wasn't sure he heard me. Moving slowly, I touched him on his forearm, making sure I made contact with his flesh and not numb tissue. He came out of his reverie, took in his surroundings and came back to me.

"It's done," he said, sheathing his knife behind his back.

Selina was dying. I didn't know who had killed her and it didn't matter. She'd failed, and now she was paying the price. It was possible she might live if she received help, but I couldn't see her step-mum forgiving her. There would be no kissing and making up. One of the two veterans went through the Yellowtails, ending their suffering, which I decided to think was an act of mercy. In reality, they were making sure none of the enemy recovered, because one day in the future, they would attempt to seek revenge.

Standing over Selina, the burly man, who was called Troy, looked down at her, not with hate or pity but disappointment.

"What?" she asked, still full of piss and vinegar. To emphasise her point she spat blood on his shoes.

Troy flipped his knife and stabbed into her neck and back out. Selina gasped and choked, the wound in her side suddenly forgotten as she struggled to breathe. Troy watched without mercy until the light faded from her eyes and she moved on to whatever came next.

Now, it was over.

CHAPTER 13

Bruised, battered and bloody, Bracken and I were struggling to stay conscious. The surviving veterans, used to dealing with wounds, patched us up as best as they could. It was crude and would leave a scar, but at least it was effective. I had a nasty gash down one thigh, a cut across my ribs and another on my right shoulder. It was only now, as the adrenaline faded, that the pain was starting to make itself known. It would get much worse over the next few hours. Bracken had a few superficial cuts that he let them tend, but otherwise was unhurt. The rest of his wounds had come from the fight he'd had with Booker. His face was still swollen and bruised. I was more worried about the damage I couldn't see, beneath his clothes. The survivors viewed him with respect that bordered on awe.

The heavy thump of footsteps, far too late, announced the arrival of the authorities. A dozen battered constables came into the corridor and then stopped, shocked by the grisly scene. Someone pushed their way to the front and the constables quickly gave way, making room for the newcomer. Even before I saw their face I knew who it was. The plush carpet muffled the sound of his boots but there was no mistaking the slight limp of Chief Langley. Coming up behind him were hawk-faced Rivera and the fresh-faced kid, Dallas.

Rivera sneered, as if this was exactly where she had expected to find me.

"You are all under arrest," said the chief. "For disturbing the peace. Yes, that will do." He nodded and gestured for the constables to take everyone into custody.

We could have fought, could have taken a few of them with us, but I didn't have the energy. And right then, all I wanted to do was lie down and go to sleep. I desperately wanted a drink as well, to numb the pain, but I didn't see that happening anytime soon. The others gave up their weapons willingly. While we were being handcuffed, someone went to fetch Mrs Dolman and the children. Before I had a chance to ask questions, two young lads grabbed me by the arm and escorted me down the stairs.

At first, I resented being manhandled by them, but by the time we reached the bottom, they were shouldering a good portion of my weight. My legs felt like jelly. My head was dizzy and my stomach began to heave. When we stepped outside, I paused to soak in some fresh air and they let me. One of them even had a small hip flask which, to my surprise, he offered. I took a short nip, wincing at the coarse burn down the back of my throat. As the heat blossomed in my stomach, Bracken and I were marched through the streets like common criminals to the police station.

They must have processed us, but I don't remember. My next clear memory is waking up in the cell, thirsty and aching from head to toe. Bracken was there and he offered me some water that someone had left for us. It tasted slightly metallic but it was cold. Exhaustion dragged me down, and hours later I woke up with sunlight playing across my eyelids. My neck was sore from sleeping at a peculiar angle, and sitting up I realised how ripe we smelled.

The cell was like all the others. Two stone shelves with a thin padded matt on top. A tiny toilet in one corner and a heavy door. The only oddity was the tray by the door with a jug of water and two battered mugs. Someone, I suspected O'Neill, had taken sympathy on us. If it had been down to any of the others they would have left us with nothing. With nothing to look at and nothing else to do, I dozed in the cell. Bracken was sitting upright but he was asleep, snoring with his chin resting on his chest.

After sleeping for a few hours, I woke sore and hungry but feeling better. Then Langley made a mistake. He left me with time on my hands and nothing to do but think. I'd been moving so fast, it was only now I had time to try to slot the pieces together.

Slowly, bit by bit, as I went over the case from start to finish, a horrible realisation dawned on me. Some might call me cynical and bitter for thinking it, but it made sense, in a twisted sort of way. And those were the kinds of people I was dealing with here.

I knew who had arranged Selina's kidnapping and I knew why.

"You've looked deeper," said Bracken, bringing me out of my reverie.

"No more straight lines," I said.

So I told him my theory. He grunted in surprise but didn't disagree.

An hour later, the cell door opened and we were escorted, by a pair of constables, to an interview room. Chief Langley sat alone behind the table and, for once, there was no sign of Rivera or Dallas. This discussion was to remain private, which didn't surprise me.

"Well, you've certainly kicked up a shit storm," said Langley, as we sat. He said nothing about our appearance nor our wounds and made no offer of medical assistance. I wasn't sure if he'd noticed. "We're doing our best to contain the situation, but it's not going to be easy. Thankfully the gang warfare was contained within the Squat Tower."

"Mrs Dolman. The children. Are they safe?"

"Does it matter?" asked the chief.

"They're innocent," I said, hoping that he still believed in something. "The kids didn't choose their parents."

Beside me, Bracken twitched but he didn't say anything. Not yet.

"They've been relocated. Somewhere far from here where no one will find them."

Langley sounded like he regretted the decision. As if someone had forced him to make it. When I'd been a cop, we'd occasionally put people into witness relocation. Usually they went to live on a farm outside New Delhi or London, a couple of hundred miles away. As the power and influence of the gangs grew in New York, witness relocation had fallen out of fashion as people became less willing to testify in public. The chief didn't sound pleased that it had been resurrected on this occasion. Mrs Dolman must have given him something juicy and he'd been forced to make a deal. Smart woman.

"Karl Dolman and the Dragons are gone. The Yellowtails are gone. I thought you'd be happy," I said.

Langley see-sawed a hand. "There's paperwork to sort. A lot of dead bodies, too. Plus, there will be fallout. A scramble for power as the other gangs try to fill the vacuum."

"So, are we under arrest?"

"No, you're here for your own protection."

"Protection from whom?" I asked.

"Everyone," said Langley with a laugh. "Half the criminal underworld wants to thank you and probably hire you. The other half wants you dead. They think you planned this from the start. That you're in league with some of the other gangs."

"But you know that's not true."

"Perhaps," he said, reminding me that he was a poor excuse for a human being. "But no one listens to me. I'm the enemy, so I'm not to be trusted."

"That much is true," said Bracken.

Chief Langley glared at him, but it was like trying to stare down a rock.

"I think it would be best for everyone if you were to leave New York for a while. It would be safer."

"And go where?"

Langley grinned. "It's funny you should ask." At that point, I realised he'd been planning this conversation for hours. "There's a case I would like you to investigate in a little township in the Wild. It's about five or six days away. I'll hire you at your normal daily rate, of course. I suspect it will take you at least two weeks, maybe a month to solve it, if you want to slow walk it." He reached into his pocket and pulled out a large stack of bills. Beside it, he placed a small, blue leather notebook. I had carried one of those for years. Every detail of every case had gone into one of those. Without looking, I knew the pages would be full of his neat script, outlining the basics of the case. Never theories, never thoughts of feelings, just the facts. "Pay up front, of course."

It sounded too good to be true. And that's because it was.

I should have just got up, taken the money and walked out.

It was only because I had known him for so long that I knew what Bracken's expression meant. Most people wouldn't notice the tightness around his eyes or the rigid angle of his shoulders. He was just as pissed off as me.

"One question," I said. "Why did it take you so long to get to Dolman's place?"

"What?" said Langley, surprised. For the first time, the conversation had veered away from his plan.

"I know you had people watching the Squat Tower," I said, not giving him a chance to respond. "So you knew all about who was coming and going. You must have seen the gang of Yellowtails going in with Selina, and yet you did nothing. Then we went in and still nothing. Since the very beginning of this case, it's felt as if I was missing something. A piece of the puzzle didn't fit with the rest and I couldn't see it."

"We were—"

"Busy elsewhere?" I said, cutting him off. "No, I don't believe that, do you, Bracken?"

"No, sir."

"I think you were hoping the Dragons and the Yellowtails would just wipe each other out. Thin the herd. Two fewer gangs for you to worry about, and if they killed some civilians in the building, well, what does it matter? My death would probably have been a bonus. You wanted a bloodbath."

"That's absurd," said the chief, but we both knew he was lying.

"One question kept rattling around in my head. Why now? Why did Selina Dolman suddenly decide to make a grab for power? What made her come up with this plan?"

Langley held himself still. I knew he was furiously trying to come up with a rational explanation. Given enough time, he would find one as well. In time, he'd probably find the evidence to support it.

"Did you know that she arranged her own kidnapping?" I asked. To give my hands something to do I grabbed the money and passed it to Bracken. He started counting the notes, splitting Langley's focus.

"It's all there," he said, annoyed that we didn't trust him to cheat us. But then, in many ways, he was just as bad as Dolman.

I took the notebook and slipped it inside my jacket for later.

"I was so surprised," I admitted. When Booker had muttered her name from between his bloody lips it had shaken me to my core. "It was all a charade to distract her father and make him look weak. He couldn't even protect his own family. What kind of a boss is that? And while he hired me, Selina was out there making deals with other gangs. Hiring the Yellowtails as muscle. She'd probably carved up her father's territory weeks ago. But then there's the question again."

Langley was starting to sweat. "What are you babbling

about?"

"Why now? And the answer is you."

The silence in the room was deafening.

At that moment, all the old hatred and loathing I'd set aside came back to the surface. I despised the man in front of me for so many reasons. This was just the latest in a long list.

"You reminded Selina that in a few years' time, her dear old dad would step down and her brother, Tony, would take the reins. But if something tragic were to happen to him, then his new family would inherit and she'd get nothing. Because she was a woman. Because she was different."

"You have no idea what you're talking about."

"Your eyes lie," said Bracken. "Your heart is cold and black."

"You did all this. I bet in a day, or two, Tony's body will be found. Was it your plan to wipe them all out? Even the kids?"

Chief Langley leaned back in his chair. A ripple of emotion passed across his face, like a pebble being thrown into a pond, and then it settled into a feral grimace. All the deep, dark emotions he held in check came boiling up.

"Do you know how many people there are living in New York City? Of course you don't and neither do I. No one does. Because people are too disorganised, and too stupid to have anything as simple as a census. There are thousands here, Cole. Tens and tens of thousands. And do you know many cops there are in the city? How many crimes we can investigate in a day? Barely any, because we don't have enough bodies. There's a rising tide of shit, and the gangs are there, stirring it all up. And right at the centre was Karl Dolman. King of the shit heap."

He was ranting. Spraying spit across the table and a part of me wondered if he was actually mad. Not the licking door handles and howling at the moon kind. The quiet, cracked in the head kind, who see the world as their own personal Hell. But then again, my outlook on humanity wasn't exactly glowing, so what did that say about me?

"The Dragons. The Yellowtails. They were two of the worst gangs, but there are dozens more and new ones springing up all the time. So I'm not going to be crying over a few less criminals on the street. In the long run, it will barely make a dent, but it might give us a moment to breathe easier and—"

"Take over their territory," I said, interrupting him. "You're nothing but another gang leader with a group of thugs."

"Get out!" he shouted.

"You're just as bad as Dolman."

"Out!" he hissed, rising from his seat. His face had gone pale and his eyes glazed over.

In the darkest hours of night, when the silence hummed in my ears and sleep just won't come, I see the faces of all of those I've failed. The victims and their families. The broken children. The desperate and the fallen. I wondered, had Langley ever experienced something like that? Or did it require a person to have a soul?

The door to the interview room opened, two constables grabbed us and we were quickly dumped on the street. We'd escaped with our lives and the case was closed. But it didn't feel like I'd won.

NEW YORK MINUTE

CHAPTER 14

Regardless of how much I hated him, regardless of everything that he'd done to foster the bloody situation we were in, Chief Langley was right about one thing. We couldn't stay in the city. I'd been too close to the Dolmans and the swirling heart of events. The repercussions would upset the underworld for a while and I needed to be elsewhere. Away from the violence that would follow. The recriminations. The revenge and carving up of the big man's territory.

But we still had time to sit, rest, recover and catch our breath.

So, after getting our wounds tended by a competent doctor, and a good night's sleep that lasted twelve hours, I found myself sipping a cold beer on Bracken's porch on a sunny afternoon. Mercifully, his miserable neighbour decided not to show her face and ruin my moment of peace.

Bracken was already busy at work, perched on a neighbour's roof, patching a hole. If we were going to be away for a while then he needed to make sure the street wouldn't fall apart in the interim. So I drank my beer, thought over the last few days, and watched him work.

When dusk began to fall, he came down, put away his tools, and joined me on the porch. We stared out at the street and beyond that, to the city that had been our home for our entire lives. We'd never left its borders. Never stepped into the Wild. I was nervous and excited. If Bracken had any opinions on our forthcoming trip, he kept it to himself. Today his face was as impassive and unreadable as stone. Even so, I could see there was something on his mind. There was a question hanging in the air.

"Say it," I said, passing him a fresh beer from the cooler.

For a while he was quiet and just picked at the label on his beer. I left him to it and eventually he found the right words. I was glad my head was turned away when he spoke because it would have been impossible to mask my fear.

"Tell me about my girls."

After swallowing the lump in my throat, I took a long pull on the beer, buying time until I was in control of my emotions.

"What do you want to know?"

Bracken put down his beer and peeled off his gloves. Even in the fading light I could see the Slate had spread across his hands. He flexed his fingers and then shook his head.

"I know it's my hand. I can see the fingers moving, but I can't always feel them. Makes the work difficult. Time was, I could work long after dusk. Now, I might hit my hand and not know it."

"What about elsewhere?"

Bracken gestured at his ribs. "It's spread a little. Here and there. But it's also changing me on the inside."

"What do you mean?"

He sighed and sipped his beer. Talking this much seemed to tax him but I waited because it needed to be said. "I lost something during the fight with the Yellowtails. Knew I was hurting people. I could see it, feel most of it too, but a part of me just didn't care." Bracken put down his beer and took out his big knife.

"What are you going to do with that?" I asked, getting ready in case he did something stupid.

"Maybe the others have it right. Maybe I should just put it through my eye now, get it over with."

"Don't. Please, don't do that. We'll work something out.

We'll find something."

Bracken offered me a rare smile. "In spite of everything, you're a rare man of faith, Cole."

"I don't believe in spirits or gods."

"I know. I didn't mean that kind of belief." With a grunt he sheathed his blade, and I heaved a sigh of relief. "I'm worried I'll lose more. How to care about others. How to be a father. What if I keep going for too long end and up like Dolman, or Chief Langley? They're cold and dead on the inside. Worse than me."

He was right. That was a risk. I wanted to tell him that everything would work out. That we'd get through it. Find a cure or some way to arrest the spread, but I didn't. Because he was my best friend and lying to him would be the worst thing. Because right now he wasn't sure what he could trust and he needed something steady and reliable. Something that wouldn't change in the coming weeks and months.

"I won't let it come to that," I said, forcing a smile, while my stomach twisted itself into knots. "I'll remind you about the important stuff. Every day."

"The girls."

"Yes."

So I told him all about the girls. Everything I could remember. From the moment they were born, to the moment they'd set off for the farm. I talked for hours. I talked until it was dark and I was tired and my throat hurt. I talked while he cooked us a couple of steaks and kept on talking around every mouthful. I talked until I was sure I had repeated some of the stories two or three times. But he didn't care and was happy to listen.

I needed Bracken to remember. I needed him to reinforce the old memories and form new ones so he didn't forget what was most precious to him. It was the only way to help Bracken hold on to his humanity, in the hope that he would stay true and continue building a better tomorrow for both of them.

STEPHEN ARYAN

ACKNOWLEDGEMENTS

The idea for *New York Minute* came to me a few years ago and it would not leave me alone. I was busy with other books, so I ignored it, but it kept nagging at me. Going in, I knew that this story didn't fit into a neat genre box, so that would make it difficult to sell. Nevertheless, I had to write it and exorcise it from my head.

Once it was drafted, I realised that because *New York Minute* was a novella, that was another barrier for most publishers. So, I sat on the book for a while (not literally). I edited it some more. I fiddled with the story a bit. I thought about if there was a way to make it into a novel. Eventually, I realised that the answer was no. I read it a few more times and I still liked it. I didn't want to just leave it on a shelf.

Given all of that, I realised that self publishing the story was going to be the best approach, but having been with my agent since 2013, and traditionally published since 2015, what did I know about self publishing? The answer was, not a lot.

Over the years, I have spoken to a lot of self published authors, and interviewed a few, but there's a world of difference between talking to someone about it, and going through the process yourself. So I called on some experts to help me who had done it, many times before.

Firstly, I want to thank my editor, Sarah Chorn. Her questions and comments were extremely helpful. Thanks to Dom, for proofreading it and helping me with those pesky commas. A massive thank you to Rachel St Clair for the cover. She presented me with several ideas, one of which was much

NEW YORK MINUTE

better than my original concept, proving once again that I'm not a visual person. Thank you to Michael R. Fletcher for patiently guiding me on the technical side. He's the reason this book looks good on the inside, and any mistakes or errors are completely my fault for ignoring him.

Thank you to all of the wonderful authors who agreed to read this and say nice things about it. Thank you also to the authors I've interviewed who have shared nuggets of wisdom with me about the self publishing process.

The final thanks has to be for you, dear reader. If you're new here, welcome. Thank you for taking a chance on an author you'd not tried before. I hope you enjoyed your time in the other New York City, on the edge of the Wild. I've written lots of other books if you want something longer. There's a list in the front.

If you're a returning reader, welcome back old friend. While this is different from my usual, hopefully you found enough that was a familiar, and you were entertained. Thank you for your continued support. I don't take it for granted.

While this is the end of one story with Cole and Bracken, there are others. Very soon, I want to take an adventure into the Wild, and I hope that you'll come along for the ride.

Stephen Aryan
October 2024

STEPHEN ARYAN

ABOUT THE AUTHOR

Stephen Aryan has been writing stories for a long time. It took him many years to find an agent, and then get his first book deal.

His debut, *Battlemage,* was published in 2015. *Battlemage* was a finalist for the David Gemmell Morningstar Award for best debut fantasy novel. It also won the inaugural Hellfest Inferno Award in France. Since then he's had ten novels published by Orbit and Angry Robot Books.

When he isn't writing, Stephen likes to spend time in the woods, pretending to be a forest ranger. Or you'll find him talking about (and drinking) real ale, watching TV, and eating copious amounts of chocolate.

Visit **www.stephen-aryan.com** for news about forthcoming books and appearances. On his website you can also sign up to his free monthly newsletter, which has advanced news about what he's currently working on.

Printed in Great Britain
by Amazon